BETWEEN THE CRACKS

STEFON MEARS

Also by Stefon Mears

The Rise of Magic Series
Magician's Choice
Sleight of Mind
Lunar Alchemy
Three Fae Monte
The Sphinx Principle
Double Backed Magic

Cavan Oltblood Series
Half a Wizard
The Ice Dagger
Spells of Undeath

Power City Tales
Not Quite Bulletproof
No Money in Heroism

Standalones
Between the Cracks
Sects and the City
Prince of a Thousand Worlds
Devil's Night
Portal-Land, Oregon
Stealing from Pirates
Fade to Gold
With a Broken Sword
Twice Against the Dragon
The House on Cedar Street
Sudden Death
On the Edge of Faerie

Short Story Collections
Spell Slingers
Twisted Timelines
Longhairs and Short Tales: A Collection of Cat Stories
Confronting Legends (Spells & Swords Vol. 1)
The Patreon Collection, Vol. 1-7 (Vol. 8, coming soon)

Nonfiction
The 30-Day Novel and Beyond!

Spells for Hire Series
Devil's Shoestring
Zombie Powder
Spirit Trap
Dragon's Blood

The Telepath Trilogy
Surviving Telepathy
Immoral Telepathy
Targeting Telepathy

Edge of Humanity Series
Caught Between Monsters
Hunting Monsters

Published by Thousand Faces Publishing, Portland, Oregon

http://1kfaces.com

ISBN: 978-1-948490-37-5

BETWEEN THE CRACKS

1

Missing, presumed dead.

Those are terrible words, aren't they? Like some authority is really saying, "Welp, we don't know where this person is, and we're not going to throw away any money looking for them. So, yeah. Let's just say they're dead, until and unless they ever show up again. Which we don't think is going to happen."

About as comforting as a bunch of politicians babbling about thoughts and prayers after some great tragedy. When you know full well that most of them were as likely to give you a hundred dollars out of their own pocket as think about you, and only ever prayed for re-election.

Yeah, don't get me started on politicians.

In this case, the person missing, presumed dead was my Uncle Charles. Good old Uncle Charles. My namesake – though technically I think we were both named after our great, great grandfather – though everyone called me Charlie. He was everything my dad warned me not to be. Irresponsible. Irrepressible. He skipped going into the family construction business. First Warren in ... seven generations to do so. Instead he...

You know, I didn't know *what* Uncle Charles used to do for

money. He was always traveling. Plus, he was hardly Dad's favorite topic of conversation, so asking questions about my uncle didn't tend to lead to answers.

Harangues and rants, yeah. Sure. But not answers.

I do remember, when I was a kid, I that I did sometimes ask Uncle Charles what he did for a living. A couple of times, at least, during visits around the holidays. But I never got anything like a straight answer out of him. Closest I can recall is one time, at Christmas, him smiling at me with eggnog-reddened cheeks, and whispering, "Having fun is my profession. But don't tell your dad." And he gave me this conspiratory wink that made eight-year-old me shiver, like I'd gotten a real secret.

Last I knew about Uncle Charles before that letter showed up was that he'd gotten his hands on a sailboat and was navigating his way around the world. According to the letter, he "disappeared" somewhere in the Caribbean.

Knowing him, probably in the Bermuda Triangle.

Apparently his boat turned up in Puerto Rico, but he wasn't on it, and some required number of weeks passed with no sign of him before some bureaucrat sent word to the Federal government. Got the process rolling. And a mere six months later they got around to informing the family. Us.

Dad read the letter with a grim, *I always knew he'd end this way* look on his face. But I swear, some of his hair got grayer overnight. Mom just shook her head sadly, and tried to take care of Dad as though he were mourning. Though if he was, he never allowed us kids to see it.

My big brother, Jonathan, he just imitated Dad's look. May have even muttered something about not being surprised. I didn't quite hear it.

Guess I was the only one who was heartbroken. Uncle Charles, he'd been a kind of hero to me. The free spirit, always with a ready smile and a story to tell. Not to mention a whole raft of other stories he'd promised to tell me when I was older.

Now I'd never hear those stories. Or see that smile again.

Almost as surprising as getting that letter from the government was getting a letter from a *lawyer* two weeks later. I mean, *none* of us suspected that *Uncle Charles* had a lawyer. Seemed way too responsible for him.

But sure enough, a Daniel McDonnell, esquire, contacted me, because apparently Uncle Charles' sense of responsibility extended to a will. Which led to the most surprising revelation of all.

Uncle Charles left me a ten-figure bank account and a little house on Portland's east side. Only two requirements: I had to live in the house on my own for at least a year – including no overnight guests for at least the first six months – and I couldn't tell the rest of my family about any of the money, beyond that he'd left me enough to handle utilities, insurance and property taxes for the first few years.

Weird, right? Very Uncle Charles, though. Especially the part about how I'd understand his reasons once I'd "gone through the house thoroughly."

Needless to say, I moved in at once.

And not just because I was nineteen, and a community college student with a freaking house of his own. No. I was *more* than happy to get away from Dad's simmering anger at my sudden announcement that I wasn't going into the family business.

Dad was the kind of man whose emotions leaked out into the world around him. When he was mad at me, it felt as though the whole house echoed his sentiment. Walls stalked. Ceilings loomed. That sort of thing.

He didn't yell at me about my decision though. Probably knew it wouldn't have helped with me any more than it had helped with his brother. Unfortunately *my* brother didn't get that lesson. Jonathan did the yelling. I let him. Figured he needed to vent. Maybe it was his own way of mourning Uncle Charles. Whatever. Jonathan yelled, and I sat there, waiting for him to finish.

Mom finally brought us in a couple of sodas. Gave Jonathan a pointed look and said, "Perhaps this will help you cool down."

Mom didn't so much as look at me askance about my big declaration. My bet is that she wasn't unhappy about it. Construction may have made a lot of money for my family, but it was pretty hard on us. Dad wasn't fifty-five yet, but he had a trick back from an unforeseeable accident, years ago, and a knee that seized up every time it rained.

In Portland.

Yeah, I figured Mom wasn't sorry to see at least one of her children find a different path. She might've been sorry to see me move out so soon – I was the baby, after all – but she didn't say anything about that either.

2

———————

Once I realized just *how much* money Uncle Charles had left me – and Mr. McDonnell implied that Uncle Charles had left me the *majority* of his estate, but not all of it – I figured this house was going to be something to see. Some kind of grand manse.

I didn't let myself look at a map before going there. The address would be easy enough to find, and I wanted to be surprised. Figured Uncle Charles would've wanted it that way. Plus, I knew the house was somewhere in the Mount Tabor district, so it might even have been on Mount Tabor itself. How cool what *that* be?

Nope. Once more, Uncle Charles had thrown me a wicked curve when I was expecting a batting-practice fastball.

It was just another little house, in a neighborhood that looked, well, *ordinary*. One- and two-story houses, all built sometime in the 70s. Postage stamp lawns, many of which had yellowed over the hot summer. Privacy fences in backyards, instead of arbor vitae.

The trees on this block were all deciduous. Fruit trees and oaks and maples and Japanese maples and magnolias. None of the Douglas firs that, growing up on the west side, I'd thought of as Portland's signature tree.

Sidewalks. Concrete driveways. Including the one I pulled my beat-up old Subaru Impreza into. Car was older than I was, but it would live a little longer yet. If I bought a new one too soon, my family might ask questions I couldn't answer.

Uncle Charles didn't leave anyone a car. Maybe he'd never owned one. Wouldn't put it past him.

Then again, living here, he might not've needed one. House might not've been much to look at. Small and simple, compared to the family home built by my great-great-grandfather, and updated with every generation since.

But the location of this little house was pretty sweet. Plenty of stores and restaurants in easy walking distance – movie theater, too – and for anything else, the MAX station wasn't more than three or four blocks away.

House was only maybe two thousand square feet, if that. Officially two bedrooms, but one was clearly used as an office for Uncle Charles' profession. Which I immediately decided had to be treasure hunting. At least, to judge by the *hundreds* of maps and notebooks filling that office. Not to mention the catalogs and binders of newspaper and magazine articles.

And I do mean *filling*, and not just the bookcases. The desk. The tables against all four walls – which had been wood-paneled, for some reason – two guest chairs, five filing cabinets... Every horizontal surface was covered with open maps, notes handwritten on cheap notebooks, and here and there a news clipping, either original or printed out. In some cases, possibly from microfiche.

The place smelled like I always imagined a newspaper's archive room would smell. Paper and ink and dust and sheer age.

I couldn't do much more than glance at that room yet. It was too much to absorb right away. So I got a vague sense of it and moved on.

The living room had a nice, big flatscreen television mounted on the wall, and a fancy soundbar with satellite speakers. But the several bookshelves lining the walls weren't filled with books or feature films on disc.

Nope. They were documentaries, on Blu Ray, DVD, Laserdisc, VHS, even Betamax. And he had players for all these things hooked up to that television. Not to mention a sixteen-millimeter projector and pull-down screen, to go with boxes and boxes of more documentaries on film.

Glancing over the titles, I had trouble understanding how he'd organized his ... collection, for lack of a better word. It was historical and anthropological stuff, mostly, but here and there were "documentaries" about UFOs and aliens, witchcraft, Satanism, Bigfoot, "cryptozoology" – whatever that was – psychic powers, secret societies and more.

No maps or notes in there, though. Maybe this was just his favorite form of entertainment? A way to unwind?

Kitchen was nice, if a bit spartan. Plenty of cutlery, glasses and dishware, but nothing in the way of pots and pans. Apparently Uncle Charles hadn't been big on cooking. Or keeping food and drinks around the house, because I found exactly zero. He'd even unplugged his nice, fridge when he'd locked up for the last time.

Thing had been unplugged for a while, too. Had that old refrigerator smell, which made me a little queasy and prompted me to close it and move on.

The bedroom had a king-size bed, bookshelves filled with paperback novels, and another wall-mounted flatscreen. This one had a streaming stick hooked up to the WiFi though.

Whatever else he was, Uncle Charles was clearly not a clothes horse. He had only one small bureau in his bedroom, and it was empty. Nothing in his closet, either. Not even hangers.

Was that odd? Well ... yes. Kind of. I mean, if nothing else, I'd expect him to keep a pair of swim trunks around to go with the hot tub I'd spotted in the otherwise simple backyard. (Hot tub was likely the fanciest thing I'd seen anywhere on the property at this point, and I was looking forward to filling it and trying it out.) But honestly, I never remembered Uncle Charles dressing up fancy. Not even when Mom dragged us all to church for Christmas Eve services.

So maybe he'd just planned to buy a new wardrobe on his trip around the world. I mean, I knew he hadn't just cleared the house out, because the linen closet was full of sheets and towels and such, and he'd left plenty of supplies in the bathroom.

Now, what I'd seen to this point felt … a little eccentric, maybe, but not all that strange. Not for Uncle Charles.

But as I returned to the living room, a wash of cold creeps swept over me. Made the hair on the back of my neck stand up.

I hadn't seen a computer in the whole house. Not one. No desktop, no laptop, no tablet, no phone. No nothing.

Closest thing to a computer I'd seen was that streaming stick in the bedroom. And I knew he had functional Wi-Fi, because, well, one, that streaming stick would be a brick if there was no Wi-Fi, and two, I was already hooked up to it.

Mr. McDonnell had given me the Wi-Fi name and password – Warrenvision and 5aturnaıia23^ – along with the keys, and I connected my phone to it first thing, on parking in the driveway. Did it without really thinking about it.

But I mean, who has *no* computers in their home these days? And for that to be true of a man as rich as he was? That was just creepy.

"What the hell, Uncle Charles?" I muttered, looking more sharply as I went through the rooms again, trying to spot anything computer-like that I might've missed. A tablet hiding under a map. A laptop stuck in a drawer or cabinet. A smart appliance in the kitchen or the laundry closet. *Something.*

But there really seemed to be nothing. No computers at all. Just…

Just physical maps, physical books, physical media for his documentaries. And tons and tons of notebooks, full of handwritten notes.

I must've stood there in the kitchen in the hot, afternoon sunlight for twenty minutes, trying to remember ever seeing Uncle Charles use a cell phone.

Couldn't do it. He never got into texting, either.

Wait! I knew he had email! I'd…

I knew I'd *sent* him email. But how did he respond? He called me. Sometimes days, or even a week later.

As though maybe he was checking his email on some public

computer. Like at the library, maybe. Or hell, his lawyer's office, for all I knew.

Did this mean Uncle Charles hadn't *owned* a computer? Of any kind? At all? Even wealthy as he was, how could he survive in modern society without a computer?

I just couldn't imagine anything weirder.

At least, not until I stepped into the garage.

3

───────────

I KNEW UNCLE CHARLES HADN'T OWNED A CAR. MR. MCDONNELL HAD already told me as much. So I'd figured the garage had to be a workshop. And given that Uncle Charles grew up a Warren, I was betting on woodworking. Give him a chance to do something with his hands, something constructiony, as a nod to the family legacy.

Yeah, I left the garage for last, because I figured that I was inheriting some big, unfinished woodworking project along with the house. And I was kind of looking forward to seeing what it was, because I knew I'd finish it.

I would've guessed a canoe, but I knew he'd already had a sailboat – technically my sailboat now, currently being sailed back to Portland by someone Mr. McDonnell had hired on my behalf – so my guess was a glider.

I was *so very* wrong.

That garage wasn't all that big. From the outside, looked as though it would only be wide enough to hold one car, although that car could've been as big as ... maybe a small motor home. And there would've been a reasonable amount of space around it, when it was parked.

But when I unlocked the side door and flipped on the garage

overhead lights all I saw were boxes and crates. Stacked up to the angled roof. So many that the Ark of the Covenant might've been tucked away in there and stayed hidden for decades.

What. The actual. Fuck.

I just stood there for a while. Slack-jawed. Coughing sometimes, from the smell of wood and cardboard and dust. Trying to let my brain make sense of what I was seeing. Because it wasn't just...

I mean, these weren't boxes stacked and shoved away to be forgotten. They were organized into clear rows, and brightly lit by track lights above each row.

Standing just inside the door, I could see no signs of wear or creasing among the cardboard boxes of that first row. No bends or folds. Which suggested that new boxes had to have replaced older boxes now and then.

What was more, every box and crate was labeled, but not in English. Hell, not using any alphabet I recognized. So not Latinate letters, nothing Cyrillic or Greek or any kind of Asian characters.

Nothing but lines and squares and dots. Had to have been some kind of secret code.

I started wandering the rows. In awe of what must've taken Uncle Charles a lifetime to put together. What could he have in here? Books? Maps? Old notebooks?

Found treasures?

I mean, if Uncle Charles was a treasure hunter, maybe this was where he...

No. That didn't make any sense. No alarm? No security guards? Yeah, the door was strong, and had an excellent lock, but it didn't look like much...

Was that the point? Were all of these treasures hidden in plain sight? Tucked away in the garage of a man who doesn't own a car, attached to a nondescript house in a nondescript neighborhood?

Maybe.

If so, some of these would be blinds. Filled with detritus or cheap *turista* crap, to distract would-be burglars. Make them think Uncle Charles was just a hoarder.

Then again, maybe he was just a kind of hoarder. I mean, that collection of documentaries, not to mention the maps, more than a little impractical...

No. The boxes and crates seemed too well organized to be the work of a hoarder. Hell, I even found a decent rolling ladder near the back of the garage, alongside a semi-electric stacker, which was kind of like a powered, pushcart forklift.

I chuckled softly. If any thief saw *that* thing, they'd know there were goods in here. I mean, the stacker alone was worth several grand.

It also went with one of the six keys on my new keyring. I already knew that others went to the desk's locking drawer, a locking filing cabinet, the house locks, and the garage locks.

Further, the presence of the ladder and the stacker proved that Uncle Charles hadn't just socked stuff away in here to be forgotten. He had a system, and he wanted to be able to get into any box or crate fairly quickly.

No way I could go back into the house without checking at least a box or two.

I closed the door, and locked it from the inside. Then I rolled the ladder around, enjoying the squeak of the wheels as something perfectly normal, picked a top box at random, scaled the ladder and unfolded the flaps.

The box I'd picked was full of manila folders. Articles about the Tunguska Blast, actual satellite photos of the area that looked to have been taken at different times, printouts of letters and reports that looked governmental – and not just our government – plus research papers, personal letters to Uncle Charles about the event, and all kinds of handwritten notes on torn-out spiralbound paper.

The notes, of course, were all written in the same code as the boxes. Squares, lines and dots, in different configurations.

I closed the box again, and glanced around the garage. So many boxes and crates. I'd have to go through all of them, too. Every one. Just like I had to go through all the maps and notes in the office. Uncle Charles would want me to.

Had to be why he insisted I live alone for the first year, and not have any overnight guests for at least six months. I'd need time to sort through all this. To begin to understand the enigma that was my late uncle.

Plus, I was *dying* of curiosity. Was this all conspiracy-theory stuff? If so, why? What did he get out of it? And how did it relate to him somehow gathering tens of millions of dollars without the rest of the family knowing?

And speaking of curiosity, where was the *basement*? Mr. McDonnell had made a point of telling me that I could not consider the house explored and understood until I'd been through the basement.

But there were no stairs in the house. No access point in the backyard that I'd seen. And nothing here in the garage either.

So where was it?

4

————

Hours later, searching for the basement entrance was still getting me nowhere. So I gave up for the day. Ran to the store so my cupboard wouldn't be bare. Changed the bedsheets and washed the old ones. Opened windows to air out the place a bit. Ordered pizza. Ate and drank to the memory of my sweet, generous, but undeniably *weird* uncle while watching "documentaries" about the fall of Atlantis, the hunt for Bigfoot, and crystal skulls.

Yes. Crystal skulls. Things that looked like actual skulls, somehow sculpted from quartz crystal by ancient peoples, for ... reasons, I guess. The documentary tried attributing to these things all kinds of cool powers, from being ancient supercomputers, to somehow recording everything that ever happened around them, to healing some guy's cat of a bald spot.

All right. I admit. My attention may have flagged a little by the time I got around to the crystal skull stuff.

Starting the next day, I tried to make sense of the office, or "map room" as I'd come to think of it. Now, I've never been a big map guy. I can read a roadmap just fine, and I can understand a political map, figure my way around an atlas and so forth.

My meager skills were no help with most of these maps. Fortunately, though, I had something on my side that apparently Uncle Charles didn't believe in: the internet.

I didn't take pictures and do image searches. That would have felt like cheating. Plus, if Uncle Charles kept all this stuff on paper and not online, maybe he had a reason for that.

I did, however, up my education on the map side of things. Discovered that spread out through the office were mostly nautical and topographic maps – though I wasn't sure how to read them yet – but some of them were of a different style. An older style. I wasn't quite sure what to make of them, except to figure they had to be nautical, because they focused largely on oceans and seas.

Their formatting wasn't consistent with modern nautical maps, though. But then, that might've been because they looked to have been drawn by hand. Certainly they weren't done to the same scale. In some cases, I wasn't sure their scale made any sense whatsoever.

I mean, yeah, here was one that had added the theoretical location of Atlantis, relative to what I was pretty sure was Greece. But the scale was just plain *stupid*. I mean, this theoretical sunken continent would've been larger than *Europe*.

How the hell could a sunken continent that size remain hidden through the centuries?

Unless maybe "Atlantis" was actually North America? Hardly consistent with the myths and legends I'd heard about Atlantis, but so what? All stories grew with the telling.

I was digging through the filing cabinets, trying to find a key to my uncle's cipher in the hope that reading the sheafs and sheafs of notes he'd left would help me understand the maps, when I realized something.

Mr. McDonnell had made very clear that this was a two-bedroom house. Which meant that this office was originally designed to be a bedroom. Which meant it *should* have had a closet somewhere.

But there was no closet. Just walls. *Wood-paneled* walls. The only room in the house with something other than textured drywall...

I started knocking on the walls until I found a stud. Then I knocked a little more until I found another. Only two feet apart. Huh. Pretty close together, especially for a one-story like this place.

Anyway, I had the stud sound fresh in my mind, and started going around the room, giving my signature triple tap – everyone in my family had a preferred stud-finding knock – every few inches. Looking for a spot where I'd expect a stud and not find one.

I found the gap I was looking for in the place that, honestly, I should've started. Inside wall between the master bedroom and this room, starting at the edge of the master's closet. Based on the sounds, the covered over closet in here was smaller. Only maybe five feet wide instead of seven like the master. But honestly, neither of them were impressive.

Still, why cover this one over? Why not use the space? And why go to such lengths to hide it? I don't just mean the wood paneling, either. Uncle Charles had set his row of filing cabinets in front of the ex-closet, further shutting it away.

The *obvious* reason to do this would be to combine the two closets for the master bedroom's use. But Uncle Charles hadn't done that. The master closet wasn't wide enough. Wasn't really deep enough, either, to make that practical. Not without giving up wall space in the master bedroom.

So why wall off this closet?

Could he have hidden something back there?

I had a sudden flash of "The Cask of Amontillado." Chuckled softly and muttered, "For the love of God, Montresor!" But I couldn't imagine Uncle Charles killing someone. Much less stashing the body in his own office closet.

So what would be the...

Stairs?

What if this room's closet had been sacrificed to make stairs down to a basement?

Heart pounding, I went quickly back to the master bedroom. Whipped open the sliding closet door. Not the left side, that led back into the hallway. And the long side would be the wall of the office. So...

I searched all along the right-side closet wall, looking for a catch of some kind.

Nothing. Though I *thought* I could detect a fine seam. Couldn't be sure, though. Might've been my imagination.

All right. All right. Slow down and think, Charlie. If the closet wall opened, there had to be hinges on one side. Not the bottom. That would lower the panel into a platform that would cover the stairs. Useless. Could be either side, or the top.

This led to another search for seams or catches or ... well, I wasn't sure, but I figured I'd know if I saw it. I even used my phone's flashlight to help, but for the life of me, I couldn't spot anything.

If Uncle Charles did his own handiwork, even Dad would've been proud of the craftsmanship.

But there had to be a way to open it. I mean, yeah, it was probably just sheetrock. I could probably punch through it if I had a mind to. But that would've ruined it. Which would've felt wrong.

Then again, sheetrock was pretty easy to replace...

I ran my hand over the panel again, trying one last time to find the catch that would open what I was convinced was a secret door, and admit me into the deepest secrets of the house Uncle Charles left me.

Nothing.

Fine.

I gave it my triple-tap to check for studs, and the whole panel swung open to the left. A motion-detector ceiling light came on, and here were concrete stairs down.

I shook my head in disbelief. *My* triple-tap was the key to opening the secret door? That means Uncle Charles must've been planning to leave the house to me when he first installed it.

Tears welled up, and I had to sit there on the stairs for a moment while the loss of my uncle washed over me once more. This had happened from time to time since we got that letter. And as I'd done the other times, I just gave myself to the sadness. I wasn't going to fight the need to mourn, the way Dad and Jonathan did.

I loved my uncle. And if, a couple of times a day, his loss over-whelmed me for a time, well, that was only human.

So I sat there on the stairs for a while. Missing Uncle Charles. Wishing he were here with me, showing me the secrets of his house. Wondering why he'd made me wait until he was gone, to share so much of himself with me.

5

After the sadness passed, I found myself thinking about my situation with a little more clarity.

I had just opened a secret panel, leading to stairs down to a hidden basement.

Did Uncle Charles file the permits for this? The updated blueprints and such? Had he let the city do its inspection, and taken care of all those other little details that make home construction projects legal?

I had a feeling he hadn't. That he hadn't wanted the presence of his basement to become general knowledge. Available to anyone who knew how to ask the right questions at the country recorder's office.

Yeah, I had a nagging feeling that Uncle Charles had done all the work himself, and been very careful about who knew that this basement existed.

Dad would call that irresponsible. But Uncle Charles, he might take the view that it wasn't hurting anyone, so it wasn't anyone else's business.

If so, that was very Uncle Charles.

It was also a very good job. The concrete stairs looked perfectly level, and just rough enough to give a little grip to shoes or bare feet.

Probably even be pretty safe if they were wet, which was often not true for concrete.

And the passageway looked finished. The walls in here weren't bare studs and insulation, but textured drywall. He'd even added a handrail.

Wouldn't call it OSHA-compliant, but otherwise, good workmanship.

The concrete was still cold under my bare feet as I started down. Stairs descended maybe fifteen feet, then bent left to the bottom landing. All concrete down here. Floor and walls both. Smooth, not rough like the stairs.

Inset in the wall before me down here was a steel door with a kick plate. Bristly, outdoor-style doormat on this side. He worried about how dirty his shoes and feet were before crossing this doorway?

The door was locked, of course. Deadbolt and handle lock.

I know it sounds like I was cool through all of this, but deep down, well, I was still a Warren. And I'd been raised to believe that construction laws and ordinances were there for a reason. That modifications to property had to be properly declared and inspected, and all appropriate fees and taxes paid on them.

That the only people who built their own secret hideaways had something *illegal* to hide.

And I still didn't know how Uncle Charles had made his money. Money he'd left to me. Money I wasn't allowed to tell my family about.

I didn't want to think bad things about Uncle Charles. He'd been a hero to me. But a lifetime of growing up in a construction family had evil whispers going through the back of my mind about all this. And they all sounded like Dad.

So yeah. My hand was shaking as I lifted the last key on my new keyring. I had a nervous perspiration going, and jumped when I heard a clicking sound up above. But a snuck glance around the corner told me that click was just the hidden door, closing.

I forced a laugh at myself. Yes, this was odd. A locked, steel door set into concrete at the bottom of a hidden staircase. And apparently I was expected to clean my feet before entering.

But what about my whole inheritance *wasn't* odd?

I took a deep, deep breath and reminded myself that I didn't have reason to think *any* of this was illegal. No matter *what* Dad's voice was saying in my head.

I still needed three tries to get the key in the deadbolt. It turned smoothly. Same key for the handle lock. Handle turned with it.

Motion detector ceiling lights came on ahead of me as I opened the door. Fluorescents. A couple of them old enough to flicker and buzz. Their harsh light showed me a hall. Narrow. All concrete. Three steel doors on each side, and another at the end.

"They're not cells," I whispered to myself. "No victims here. Just ... stuff he doesn't want people to find. Maybe he'd really just been a treasure hunter. Maybe this is where he stored his most valuable booty."

I wasn't convinced, though. My sphincter kept clenching. My knees jittered. My stomach was jumping around like that breakfast of leftover pizza had been a mistake, and not just because I was burping garlic and pepperoni. I wanted to know what was in these rooms, but I was worried that I didn't *really* want to know.

That maybe Uncle Charles had been such a mystery because he *did* have something to hide.

Seven doors to all my answers.

The logical thing to do would be to go through each pair of facing doors as I came to them, and leave the far door for last.

Screw that.

I scraped my feet across the rough bristles of the doormat. Then, shoulders back in an attempt to force confidence I didn't feel, I marched straight down the hall to the door at the end.

There was no lock on it! I sighed *hard* as I sagged in relief. Of course there was no lock on it. No reason to lock a door behind a locked door behind a secret door. At least, not unless there was some kind of captive behind it...

But I could stop that line of thinking now. Because this door couldn't be locked.

A few heavy breaths and anxious chuckles later – well, and a head rush I had to ride out – I finally opened that door at the end of the hall.

No motion-detector lights inside. I had to find a switch on the wall, which lit up track lighting that circumnavigated the squared ceiling, washing the room in soft white light.

The room was a concrete cube, maybe twenty feet on a side. Center of the room was open, except for a series of odd designs painted on the floor in blacks and reds. Geometric shapes and words that weren't English. Around the perimeter were several tall, broad wooden cabinets surrounding a matching armoire. All of them pale woods that looked like they came from some furniture chain. Maybe that big Swedish one, which would piss Dad off. Family policy was to buy local whenever possible.

Matching desk on another wall, but it was thick with drawers. Like an old-timey teacher desk, but with a roller chair tucked in. Huge, handmade bookcase next to it. Easily eight feet tall, and half again as wide. Not quite stuffed to the gills, but pretty darned full. And no mass market paperbacks in here. Lots of hardbacks, some of which looked seriously old and leatherbound.

Another, smaller bookcase on the other side of the desk. And this one looked to be stuffed with notebooks.

But what really drew my attention was the single slip of paper lying on the desk.

I walked around the perimeter of the room on my approach. Just felt respectful, considering I didn't know what those designs were, or why they were there.

I picked up the letter. Not only was it written in English, instead of his cipher, but it was addressed to me!

Well, what else could I do but sit and read it?

6

DEAR CHARLIE,

If you're reading this, I'm either dead or missing. Given the kinds of places I go, that's always a risk.

First off, congrats on being as clever as I think you are. You found my real office. Now, first thing you should know is this. If any of the captives in the other rooms get restless...

I'm kidding! No captives. Despite what your father thinks, some of us build secret things for reasons that are nobody's damned business but our own.

And I do mean "our," because as of this moment, my secrets are yours too.

Now. Before I go any further, I want you to stop, close your eyes, and take three deep breaths. Big, belly breaths, like I taught you. Relax your face, your shoulders, your belly, and then take three breaths, just as deep as you can, and let each one out slowly. Then I want you to just feel the room. The air. However you want to think of it. Think about what it feels like to you. Right this moment.

Yes, I really want you to do this. Right now, please.

I sighed, but did as he asked. I felt the same chill I'd felt since I came down the stairs, but that only stood to reason. I was underground and surrounded by concrete. Of course it was cooler down here. Air could've been a little fresher, but if there was anything else, I couldn't feel whatever he wanted me to feel.

So I started reading again.

Truth now. Hairs on the back of your neck stand up? Maybe a sense that someone's watching you? Maybe a sense of presence coming from that little circled triangle in the far corner of the room, past the cabinets?

I immediately looked over there, but saw nothing. And although I *now* my shoulders kind of itched as though someone was watching me, I hadn't felt that way a moment ago. At least, I didn't *think* I had.

I went back to reading.

Don't overthink it, Charlie. If you felt it, you'd know. You wouldn't doubt.

Now. If you did, well, I don't know how to tell you this, but I'm not dead. And I'm going to need you to open the top, righthand drawer of the desk and read the contents of the envelope marked, "In case I'm alive."

I'm going to continue on, though, as though you hadn't felt anything like that.

Sorry, buddy, but if you had any doubts, you can let go of them. I'm dead, and I've moved on. Which means all of this is yours.

The sheer certainty of that statement hit me like a blow to the stomach. My knees folded. I could hear my pulse pounding in my ears, and my face got hot.

He wasn't just missing. He was dead.

Wait. How could he know that? Just because *I* didn't feel any creepy sensations while standing down here? That's some kind of proof?

Ridiculous.

I went back to the letter.

Sorry, buddy, but if you had any doubts, you can let go of them. I'm dead, and I've moved on. Which means all of this is yours.

Of course, you're probably wondering what comprises "all of this." Doubtless you've seen my map room, my documentaries, and possibly even the garage.

It's simple, Charlie. Your father and I were raised to be practical. Keep your head down. Do your work. No time for frivolity or fantasy.

Well, I'm pretty sure you know I said "fuck that" at an early age. What you probably didn't know was that I decided to pursue every frivolous, fanciful thing I could think of. Cryptozoology, psychic powers, paranormal phenomena... You name it, I've probably chased it down, looking for the kinds of truths that would drive my father mad.

I've found a bunch of them, Charlie. Oh, don't get me wrong. I've hit plenty of dead ends and seen more than my share of bullshit. But I've also found truths you wouldn't believe.

And one of them – the biggest one, in my opinion – is magic.

Not stage magic. But not fantasy wizards throwing fire and raising castles with a spell, either. No, I've found the real thing. Practiced at least as far back as ancient Greece and Egypt, and following the same basic structure ever since.

I've learned how to conjure spirits, Charlie. And how to compel them to do things. Like, say, find the current location of a lost shipment of Wells Fargo gold from the gold rush days. You know. Just as an example.

Anyway, you're standing in the office where I do it. Or most of it, anyway.

Now, I've left you not that far shy of a hundred million dollars. That's a pretty good nest egg. And I want you to enjoy it. Live. Do all the things you've ever wanted to do. And if you have no interest in magic and the kinds of weird things that fall through the cracks of what science can currently explain, then you can just wall this room off. Sell all the grimoires to your left. They'll fetch a good price. But burn my private notebooks. The ones to your right. Because if you aren't going to use them, I want them to follow me to my grave.

But if you're as much like me as I think you are, you're at least curious enough to find out more. And if you are, start with the first two notebooks on the top shelf to your right. The ones closest to you.

The first will teach you my cipher. I strongly suggest you study it until you've mastered the code before you do anything else. And don't bring that notebook out of this room. We mustn't risk anyone else finding it. Because in that notebook, after the key, is a complete catalog of everything in the garage, by row, column, and box/crate number.

All sorts of goodies in the garage. Some of which are protected in ways you wouldn't understand yet.

The second notebook will get you started, learning about magic. A personal guide for you, if you will, culled from my own studies and experiments. Plus, an annotated reading list, about which of those grimoires to your left you should read, and in what order.

Don't rush. Take it slow. Focus on every step. Don't do this halfway, Charlie. Take this seriously, and whole worlds will open up for you. The most amazing wonders. But if you're not interested enough to really put the work in, then just sell the grimoires, burn my notebooks, and wall off this room.

I mean it. Half-ass this and you could open yourself to all kinds of trouble. But if you put the work in, you'll do well.

Whatever you do, Charlie, live a good life. It'll be over before you know it.

Love,

Uncle Charles

P.S. Don't read any kind of prognostication into my leaving you this letter. I leave it every time I travel. Just in case.

7

———

I MUST'VE SAT THERE, READING THAT LETTER OVER AND OVER, FOR AT least an hour.

Magic. Uncle Charles was claiming he'd found real magic. That he'd actually summoned spirits, and...

Wait. Did that mean the dead? Or demons? Or what?

Oh, what did it matter? The thought that Uncle Charles could conjure up *any* kind of spirits, it just seemed impossible.

But on the other hand, the money was very real. I certainly couldn't deny that.

I also couldn't just *accept* all this. It was too wild. Too far out there.

I pulled out my cell phone. No reception down here, of course. Not surrounded by all this concrete.

So I trucked back up the stairs to the master bedroom and called Mr. McDonnell. His assistant patched me right through, and in moments I was listening to his deep, rich voice.

"Charlie! Good to hear from you. Is there something I can help you with?"

"This may sound kind of strange."

"That's fine, Charlie," he said, and from his tone he was really saying that he *expected* me to have a strange question or two.

"Do you know what my uncle did for a living?"

"Of course."

"What?"

"He was a remarkably successful treasure hunter, Charlie. Good enough to eschew publicity, and work from the shadows, as it were."

"Do you *how* he was so successful?"

Mr. McDonnell's pause seemed to carry a physical weight. But finally he spoke.

"Shall I interpret that question to mean that you've found the basement?"

My mouth went dry. I had to work some saliva into it before I could say anything.

"I have."

"Then I believe you already know the answer to your question. Don't you?"

I didn't know how to answer that. Mr. McDonnell seemed such a stolid, practical man. And to hear implications that *he* knew my uncle was ... what ... a real-life wizard? That made it all both less real and more real at the same time.

"Charlie, have you read much Shakespeare?"

"Let me guess," I said with a sigh. "'There are more things in heaven and earth, Horatio, than are dreamt of in your philosophy.' Right?"

"Perhaps applicable, but I was thinking rather of a quote from *Henry IV*. 'I can call spirits from the vasty deep.' 'Why so can I; or so can any man. But will they come when you do call for them?'"

"You're saying they came when my uncle called for them?"

"I'm saying that results speak for themselves, Charlie. And that I suspect you have some reading to do."

I nodded, not thinking about the fact that he couldn't see me. But Mr. McDonnell's voice was quiet and urgent when he spoke again.

"Charlie, I do need to know something. Did you feel watched? In the basement?"

The question shook me out of my reverie.

"No," I said, but before I could finish my thought, the heaviness of Mr. McDonnell's sigh distracted me.

"He really is dead then." He muttered something I couldn't quite hear. A blessing maybe, but it didn't sound like English.

"But how can you know that?" I asked quickly. "What was all that about? Asking me if I felt the creeps, and if not, he must be dead? Like that's some kind of *proof*?"

"It's not about "creeps," Charlie," Mr. McDonnell said. "It's about ... well ... I'm not sure you're ready to understand this part."

"Try me."

"I'd like to. But my answer won't make sense to you. Not yet. Not until you've studied for a time."

"Mr. McDonnell, you just told me that my uncle is definitely dead. Not just missing. I think I deserve to know how you can be so certain."

He drew in a breath deep enough to suck the air out of a small room, and I found myself wondering if he was doing the same kind of relaxation breath Uncle Charles taught me.

"All right, Charlie," he said softly. "I'll try you. While your uncle was alive, his familiar guarded his workshop. Now, his familiar would recognize you and allow you access, but you would have felt its presence. Felt it watching you. Does that make sense?"

"His ... familiar?"

"That's right."

"Like a witch's cat?"

"Not in the least. But as the room felt empty to you, the familiar had to be absent. Which would not be true, were your uncle still alive."

"This ... familiar. It would be one of the spirits my uncle called up?"

"Not quite. And I'm afraid that any further attempts at explanation will only lead to more questions. Do your reading, Charlie. You'll find your answers."

That was pretty much the end of *that* phone call.

I took a break. Went into the kitchen for some soda. Made a sandwich. Turkey and Swiss on whole wheat. At least, that's what I *think* it was. I was kind of befuddled. My mind was spinning at the implications of ... well ... everything.

On the one hand, every aspect of my upbringing said this was all ridiculous. Magic? Spirits? But on the other, Mr. McDonnell was right. There was no more practical proof than results, and Uncle Charles had certainly gotten those. In spades.

Of course, I didn't know anything about treasure hunting, either. Maybe he'd just gotten lucky one time. Like playing the lottery. Possibly even with better odds. I didn't really know.

But Uncle Charles had never been a *liar*. Yeah, he'd had fun with me when I was a kid. Games of make believe and so on. But he'd never lied to me. He'd refuse to tell me things. He'd tell me to ask my parents. He'd distract me from the subject. He'd talk around answering. But he never directly lied.

Even when I asked him if Santa was real, when I was five years old. He hadn't just said yes, like most adults would've. He'd said, "Didn't you get presents from him last year?" And when I'd nodded, he'd chuckled and added, "Then why doubt him now?"

Five-year-old me couldn't see a flaw in that logic, and Uncle Charles distracted me from further analysis with a game of catch.

But Uncle Charles had been both direct and explicit in that letter. Magic was real. He could conjure and compel spirits.

And Uncle Charles didn't lie to me. Which meant he believed it. Which meant he was either insane ... or right.

Even weirder, stable, solid-seeming Mr. McDonnell appeared to believe it all too. His sadness had seemed genuine when I told him I hadn't felt any sense of presence in my uncle's office.

That business about familiars...

When I tried to drink from an empty glass, I realized noon was long past. I suddenly became aware that I was sweating in the hot afternoon sun, which streamed in through the kitchen windows. I could barely taste the remains of my sandwich.

I'd been sitting there far too long. Trying to puzzle through it all.

Find some way to make logical sense out of the most illogical thing I'd ever heard. Familiars. Magic. Spirits.

If all this was true, why didn't everyone know about it? Why wasn't it taught in schools?

All right. No. I could understand that much. If it's illegal to pray in school, it *has* to be illegal to summon up spirits. And how much worse would bullying be if everyone could call up bigger and badder demons and sic 'em on each other.

Life would be a videogame.

But there had to be a middle ground, didn't there? Something between 'kept secret from the world at large' and 'taught in every grade school?'

If it was all real.

This was too much for me to deal with right then. I couldn't get my head around it. Shelved the question for now. Set down my empty glass. Stood up.

There were six other rooms downstairs. I had to go through them. See what there was to see. And then, well, I knew I definitely wanted to learn Uncle Charles' cipher. Needed to understand the contents of the garage. Not to mention all the notes he'd left in the map room.

Without meaning to, without really thinking about it, I wandered into the living room. Stared up at the wall of documentaries. At least *they* made sense now. Sort of. Anyway, I understood why they were there. What Uncle Charles was looking for from them.

He'd dedicated his whole life to finding the secrets that fell between the cracks. Every one of these tapes and discs and films, something he'd pursued. Looking for truth.

I shook my head.

The documentaries could wait. The map room and garage, too. Those six other rooms, they came first. Then the cipher and the garage. Then ... we'd see.

8

———————

Having dithered as much as I reasonably felt I could, I girded myself and went back down the stairs.

I hadn't locked the basement door behind me when I came up to call Mr. McDonnell. I resolved not to let that happen again. The secrets down here, Uncle Charles clearly didn't want me sharing them with anyone. And I didn't understand enough yet to consider overruling him.

For that matter, going forward, I decided to be more circumspect in what I discussed with Mr. McDonnell. He seemed to be Uncle Charles' friend as well as his lawyer – enough to put forth at least a *show* of sorrow at his passing – but apart from that familiar thing, I didn't know how much he knew.

And Uncle Charles hadn't told me to go to anyone else with my questions.

So I opened the heavy, steel basement door and thought about closing it behind me, but not yet. Not this time. The air down here needed some freshening.

The motion detector lights came on above the stark hallway. With all that concrete and those steel doors, it still looked like a horror-movie set. I had to remind myself that it wasn't. It was just a part of my home. A part of my legacy from my strange, beloved uncle.

I tried the first door on my left. No lock.

I swung it open. Found and flipped the light switch.

A torchiere lamp came on, lighting up an empty cube of a room. All right, not *quite* empty. I mean, there was the lamp, and a square of gray rug in the center of the room. No. Not a rug. A yoga mat, maybe? Except that it was square, maybe three feet on a side.

Weird choice. Even the lamp looked like an afterthought, plugged into one of six outlets. Cheap thing, probably just snatched quickly at a store, so there'd be light in here if Uncle Charles needed it.

Though what he wanted with a square yoga mat, I had no idea.

I left the door open and tried the door across from it.

This room was *almost* empty. But a torchiere lamp light up when I flipped the switch, and the light showed me a...

Something.

It looked like a box on wheels. Brushed steel. Big vents.

A closer look got me my answer. An air purifier. Great big, industrial strength version. Probably could freshen the air of the whole basement, if the doors were left open for a while.

I chuckled and turned it on. It rumbled loudly to life and made a sucking sound.

I left it to its task. Closed and locked the basement's entry door, but resolved to leave all the other doors open until the air purifier finished its job.

On to the second set of doors. Left hand side first. No locks here either, or on any of the other doors.

This room had a motion-detector light, so as soon as I opened the door I knew I was looking at a workshop. Workbenches lined the walls. Cabinets mounted on the walls above them, and chests of drawers underneath. All of the furniture strong. Heavy. And made from a pale hardwood that I was pretty sure was ash.

Starting my survey of the room under what looked to be a ventilation hood, I found a small forge and crucible and equipment for casting, along with a tiny anvil for small scale forging. Uncle Charles must've done jewelry smithing.

Yep. In drawers, I found ingots of gold, silver, copper, tin, iron, steel and a few other metals.

But that wasn't all. He had handheld power tools that allowed him to do more of his own small-scale wood and metalwork in here as well. Not to mention engraving, etching, and woodburning.

Weirdest part? The sewing machine in the corner. I mean, doing his own jewelry smithing, metalwork and woodwork? Sure. I could see that. Made some sense for a Warren to lean that direction. But sewing? Where did that come in?

Still puzzling about that, I crossed the hall and opened the next door.

No motion detector lights in here. No light switch either. Had to turn on my phone flashlight to see...

A library?

Tall bookshelves all along the walls. Thick, Persian carpets on the floor. A big leather recliner in the center of the room.

But no lights?

Wait. Candles. In sconces all around the room, plus a candelabra on a side table next to the recliner.

Fortunately, there was a box of matches beside the candelabra. I went around the room lighting candles, then turned off my phone's flashlight. The glow of the candleflames was soothing, even with the rumble and suck of the air purifier coming in through the open door. I slowly became aware of the pleasant smell of beeswax.

Now I could see more comfortably that my uncle had a much larger library of weirdness than just one bookcase of grimoires. No, he had shelves and shelves of books about magic from all around the world. And not just magic. This room was like the library equivalent of the documentary wall upstairs.

Psychic powers and the paranormal. Loch Ness and Bigfoot and the yeti. Aliens, both sightings and reputed abductions. Weird places, strange events, and more. Much, much more, from all around the world.

Including at least three books I spotted about crystal skulls. But man, I'd believe in *magic* before I'd believe in ancient supercomputers that just happened to look like skulls shaped out of quartz crystal.

I mean, there are *limits*, you know?

One thing I didn't find in that room? Power outlets. Didn't look as though Uncle Charles had wired this room at all. But why would that be? Even his magic office had the track lighting around the edges. Why wouldn't his library?

I extinguished the candles, left the door open, and went down the hall to the last set of unopened doors.

My pulse raced. My heart pounded hard in my chest. And I couldn't figure out why I felt so nervous. Why I felt so jumpy.

Maybe I was just worried about what kinds of secrets I'd learn next.

I opened the left-hand door.

No lights in here either. With a sigh, I went back to the library for the box of matches, then changed my mind. Lit the candelabra – six thick white candles – and carried it with me, trying not to feel as though I'd just taken that final step into one of those old Hammer horror films. All I'd need was to find Christopher Lee sleeping in a coffin.

When I saw the coffin, I dropped the candelabra. Three of the candles went out, but by the flickering light of the other three, I stood, staring at the white coffin. It looked to be set up against an altar of some kind.

I grabbed the loose, fallen candles, and got them all lit and back in the candelabra. Inhaled deep of the beeswax, to calm myself, and tried to make sense of the room.

I started with the coffin. A white coffin, draped with a black cloth. Some kind of snake and cross logo on the cloth. Beside the head of the coffin, a round white table that had to be an altar. It had an incense censer, a black-handled dagger, a smooth wooden stick – wand, I guessed – a black disc, a crystal chalice, and another disc marked with a pentagram.

Holding my breath, I opened the coffin.

Empty.

Relief hit so hard I got a headrush and sank gratefully to the tile floor.

Tile floor?

I finally realized there was more to the room than the coffin and altar. The floor was tiled in black, with a great big star done in white across the tiles, with words and symbols worked around the lines. A tall, iron candlestick holding three thick, white pillar candles at each point of the star. One point of the star at each vertex of the seven walls.

Yes. Seven walls. And every inch of them covered in one-foot-square tiles of different colors, each marked with a magic symbol of some kind.

Looking up, I saw that the ceiling was like a negative reflection of the floor. White, with a black star and black symbols and lettering.

Whoa.

If that room at the end was where my uncle did most of his magic, just what did he do in here?

Shaking my head in wonder, I crossed the hall to the last unopened door. I threw it open, glad to have the candelabra, because this room had no electric lights either.

After that last room, this one was a comedown.

A circle on the floor, and a triangle. A few tables whose tops were entirely marked up with magic symbols, and another that held a wax disc completely engraved with more symbols. Candles on the tables, an honest-to-god crystal ball, a couple of rune-graven wands. Four colored banners on the walls. Black, white, red and green, each with a different magic symbol.

All right. What did this mean? If my uncle did "most" of his magic in that room at the end, his office, then this room and the one across from it had to be for magic of very specific types.

And *damn* if I didn't want to know what these two rooms were used for.

But I would stick to my plan. I would learn my uncle's cipher. Figure out what all was in the garage. *Then* decide what to do about all the rest.

9

———

Took me two days to master the cipher to the point that I could read and write it without thinking about it. I told myself that was fast, but honestly I didn't know. On the one hand, it seemed like a pretty simple cipher. On the other, I knew my uncle pretty well, and the cipher kind of felt like him. If that makes any sense.

Even if it does, I have to say, having learned it, I felt even closer to him.

Helped that in that first notebook, after the cipher key (and Uncle Charles had even left exercises to speed my learning of it), but before the garage catalog, he left me a page devoted to a little note.

Good work, Charlie. You now have the key to all my secrets. Use them well.

On, then, to the contents of the garage, which broke down along three lines.

Ten percent: detritus. Useless stuff that might look like lost artifacts or research material, but really was just junk.

Eighty percent: additional notes and research material from his lifetime of peering between the cracks of reality. Stuff I'd probably want to go through at some point, but low priority.

Ten percent: treasures he hadn't sold yet. Most of those were old forms of money. Spanish doubloons. Coins from ancient Rome or Byzantium or Damascus. Scrip – or money, depending on how you look at it – printed by Emperor Norton or the Confederacy. That sort of thing.

But there were also a few genuine artifacts that he'd found one place or another. And *those* I felt a little antsy about. I mean, I couldn't just *sell* them. They weren't like old money. They were tools and artwork. Part of some country's history. I'd have to find a way to return them to their proper governments. Or, even better, directly to one of their museums.

I'd just need to figure out how to do that without having to answer a bunch of awkward questions, or attracting the kind of publicity – not to mention governmental attention – I *really* didn't want.

Maybe the key to that was staying local? Museum curators these days had to be pretty straight-shooters, when it came to their own fields of interest, didn't they? And likely to have contacts around the globe? Heck, they could even claim all the "glory" for the discovery themselves, if they wanted it. And they were more than welcome to any rewards. Not like I needed the money.

Digging around about local museums and their curators would be a side project, though, while I continued working my way through everything Uncle Charles had left me.

The map room came next.

Making sense of that took a week solid of my picking at it day and night. But then, Uncle Charles hadn't organized it with me in mind. Heck, he hadn't *organized* it at all. It was a scattershot mess of notes and maps that had made perfect sense to *him*, because he already knew what he was doing and why he was doing it.

By the end, though, I had to go back downstairs and double-check my understanding of Uncle Charles' cipher. Because what I was reading made not much more sense than this whole magic-is-real business.

Uncle Charles had been trying to track down a lost shipment of *orichalcum*. Maybe you're wondering what that means. I know I was, when I first ran across the word. Orichalcum can mean two things.

One of them is a kind of bronze alloy used in coin-making in ancient Rome.

The other is purely the stuff of myths and legends. It was a kind of gold-like metal mined in *Atlantis.*

That's right. Atlantis. Which explained some of the archaic, hand-drawn maps I'd found that depicted where Atlantis was supposed to have been.

When Uncle Charles had died, he hadn't been looking for the lost continent of Atlantis. He'd been looking for a shipment of mythic metal *from* that continent and bound for Athens.

Puerto Rico must've been his last port of call before heading east across the Atlantic in search of his lost shipment.

But all he'd had was a sailboat. No way he was taking a *sailboat* to hunt down lost treasure from some wreck on the ocean floor. He'd need way too much equipment. Plus, he'd been alone. And he couldn't possibly pull a wreck from the ocean floor by himself.

Was magic the answer? Was raising the treasure from a sunken wreck something his spirits could do for him?

Rather than leaping to conclusions, I dug back into his notes and came to a different conclusion.

Oh, he *was* trying to track a wreck that was supposedly carrying a shipment of orichalcum from Atlantis to Athens. I'd gotten that much right the first time. But I'd jumped the gun when I'd thought he was off trying to raise a wreck. He'd been trying to gather information. Maybe figure out what the route had been, or if there were any other stops the ship had to make on its way to Athens.

At least, that was the most sense I could make out of his notes that he needed "links," and that he had ideas about where to find the "best ones."

Unless this had something to do with chains, and I didn't think it did, Uncle Charles must've needed more information so he could make "connections" that would help him track the wreck. Like linking things together.

Unfortunately, that was about all I could make out of what I found in the map room. Or at least, what I could determine from the way he'd left it. There were a lot more maps and notes, but I didn't think they had any reason to be related. They were scattered about like the ones I'd gone through, and hadn't been referenced in the loose notes.

It seemed that my uncle had met his end doing what he loved. Looking for treasure. So I could at least take some comfort in that.

But I had also done all the vacillating I reasonably could. The cipher, the garage, the map room. Now I understood all of those things. Which left the one big question.

Was I going to try studying my uncle's magic?

Just the question set my stomach twitching. Made my breaths a little shaky. Even thinking the question made me want to look around to see if anyone was watching me. Even though the curtains of the map room were drawn tight.

Clearly I was afraid. And that decided it.

One thing both Dad and Uncle Charles agreed on – a man had to face his fears. And I didn't know whether I was afraid that magic was real or that it wasn't. If it wasn't, then my uncle had been insane. A genius, at least as a treasure hunter, but insane.

But if it was, what was it Uncle Charles had said in his letter? "Whole new worlds" would open up for me.

Well, time to find out.

I went into the master bedroom closet, opened the hidden door, and went downstairs to start learning whatever exactly it was that Uncle Charles had written in that bookcase full of notebooks.

10

WELL, UNCLE CHARLES HADN'T BEEN KIDDING ABOUT TELLING ME TO take my time. First thing he had me doing was learning to freaking meditate.

I didn't see how that could be one of the great secrets of the universe. I mean, meditation was everywhere these days. It was practically a pop subculture unto itself. Like running. One internet search showed me thousands of gushing converts, extolling all the wonderful ways their lives had changed by taking up this one practice.

Honestly, I was pretty sure that pulling a find/replace on most of those gushers would prove that there were only maybe fifteen such articles in existence. They just got reused with names and little details changed, or maybe the old fad replaced by the new one.

Which maybe made it appropriate that Uncle Charles wanted me to take up another such practice that grew the gushers. Running. Not on a treadmill, either. No. He specifically instructed me to go out into the world each day, to run.

With the meditation, he left a chart that started small – five minutes, once a day, and would progress over the course of a few months until I was meditating for thirty minutes, twice a day.

With the running, he broke it down by distance, translated for me into steps. Likely because he knew I had a smartwatch that counted for me. Again, starting small – a half-mile a day – and built up over the course of months to five miles a day.

Not exactly what I expected on learning that Uncle Charles intended to teach me his magic. But he insisted that these were two of the foundational pillars that would support everything else.

Well, I promised myself I'd take this seriously. That I wouldn't half-ass it, as he'd warned me against doing in that letter. (Which I read nightly before bed for the first couple of weeks. Just as a touchstone.)

As a good student, I started following my regimen of running and meditation, starting small and building from there. Which, fortunately, left most of my day free. So I was also able to maintain something of a social life, and attend my History and Language classes, when the semester started. (Though I switched my language study from Spanish to Latin, because the notebook recommended learning it.)

I even stopped by the house once in a while to say hi to Mom, and try to make peace with Dad and Jonathan. Though no dice on the latter. Not yet. Dad saw me as his brother 2.0, and Jonathan, well, I wasn't sure if he was angry because Dad was or if he'd honestly wanted to work with me in the family business.

I was betting on the former. Jonathan and I had never been all that close. At the same time, though, I was starting to get used to surprises about what was true and what wasn't...

After the first few weeks of running and meditation, the notebook added a third "foundational pillar" to my daily routine: visualization exercises. Apparently with a goal of getting me good at imagining clearly with all my senses.

I have to admit, it was the visualization exercises that almost lost me. The meditation, well, I had to admit that I was living more in the present, and getting better at recognizing when I was getting angry, or when I was holding on to emotions about something – say, someone cutting me off on the freeway – that served no purpose.

I was even getting pretty good at letting go of useless emotions and fruitless lines of thought once I recognized them. So, yeah, I had trouble arguing with the meditation aspect.

And the running, too. Oh, I wasn't ready to write one of those gushing blog posts or anything, but I had to admit. I was sleeping better. I had more endurance. I was trimming down and feeling good.

The visualization stuff, though. I just *could not* see the point of it. Who cared if I could clearly imagine every step of a walk around the block, including the traffic sounds and exhaust smells, the hum of a MAX train in the background, the taste of the late summer air, and the feel of the sun on my skin?

I mean, I *couldn't* do all those things yet. Not in any detail. But sitting there for a half-hour at a stretch trying to imagine with my different senses was *wearing* on me something fierce. Wasn't like with meditation, where I could get lost in my breathing and not care that time was passing. With the visualization exercises, my mind kept trying to wander.

I'd find myself wondering what step would come next. And how I'd know when I'd gotten good enough. Not necessarily *good*, but good *enough*. And maybe how long it was until dinner. And whether or not I should've done my class homework before settling down to *this* homework. And on and on.

My options were to struggle through it or quit. And I was getting seriously close to quitting.

Ironically, it was Jonathan who kept me at it.

It had been a long autumn day. The pouring rain had stolen most of the fun from my run. My paper on the War of the Roses only got me a B. Not even a B+, a B. And in Latin, I was having trouble with the third declension.

I was due to go downstairs for my visualization exercise. So when my cell phone rang, I answered, even knowing it was Jonathan, who was most likely calling to yell at me.

Any delay sounded like a good delay at that point.

So I sat in the cool, gray sunlight of my kitchen and answered.

"What's up, Jonathan?"

"I've been doing a lot of thinking lately, and I want to thank you."

"Thank me?" I asked, careful as a bomb defuser.

"Yes, thank you. Honestly, Charlie, the more I think about it, the more I realize you've done the whole family a favor."

"By moving out? What, have you already repurposed my old room?"

"No, Dad did that. It's his home office now. No, it's just that I've come to terms with the fact that you were always going to quit on us."

"Oh?"

"Inevitably. And really, it's better that you quit now, when you'd barely gotten your construction feet wet. Much better than waiting until we've come to rely on you, and leaving us scrambling."

"Is *that* how you see it?" My voice was getting hot with anger. Of *course* I'd planned on going into the family business. The whole point of my coming to college was to get a degree in Business so I could help Warren Construction expand and thrive.

"Well, that's your history, isn't it? You quit Little League after only one year."

"I sucked. I couldn't hit two hundred. In *Little League.*"

"Yes, and heaven forbid you go to the batting cages for extra practice, or even ask Dad to help you. Which he would've. No, you quit. Like you quit piano."

"That was about the *teacher*. I couldn't stand that asshole."

"Did you keep at it on your own? Did you ask for a new teacher? No. You didn't. You quit. Anytime something gets tough, you quit. And now Uncle Charles gave you an easier path than working for the family – and I don't buy this bullshit about him only leaving you enough money to cover bills for a while, he must've gotten lucky in Vegas or something – and what do you do? You quit."

My skin was hot. My heart was pounding. Fury screamed through my veins.

But meditation, it had given me tools to deal with situations like this. I realized in that moment that what I was feeling was only *masking* as anger. Because it was shame. Shame that my brother was absolutely right.

I quit Little League rather than put the work in and learn to hit.

I quit piano, because trying to keep at it on my own was harder than working with even a bad teacher.

That wasn't why I'd quit the family business, but it was a reasonable conclusion. And since I'd promised not to tell my family about the money, I couldn't tell him my real reasons.

Clarity stole the power from my shame. My failures, my quitting, that was shameful behavior all right. Was. As in, in the past. But this conversation, this was happening *now*. This second. With me sitting all tight and tense in my kitchen, clutching my phone to my ear. This wasn't eight-year-old me with baseball, or twelve-year-old me with piano.

I was eighteen. Almost nineteen. And I was not a prisoner to my past. Every moment, every second in life, was a chance to change my ways. To pick a new path for myself.

And I would do just that.

Starting with a few of my uncle's belly breaths, to unclench my muscles and calm my speeding heart.

Jonathan was still ranting when I tuned back in.

"...And when Uncle Charles' money runs out and you're working some shit job for shit pay, don't come crying to me for something better. Because I'll treat you just like any other new applicant. And you won't have any experience to back you up. You won't—"

"You're right," I said.

"—be the best candidate, and you'll be lucky if I can find you..." Silence for a moment, apart from worked-up breathing. But I didn't interrupt him. "What did you just say?"

"I said, 'You're right, Jonathan.'"

The tension in his silence was like a physical compulsion to keep talking. I could just picture him. Three inches taller and fifty pounds of muscle bigger than me, and every inch and ounce of him wire-tight with anger and distrust while he waited for me to continue.

He'd grown his bangs too long again. They'd be dangling past his bushy eyebrows, framing his vision like brown straw from a wide-brimmed hat.

He was sitting in his truck. His fancy F-150, with the leather seats. Smelling the Douglas fir air freshener that dangled from his rearview mirror.

"I do have a pattern of quitting when it gets tough," I said. "In fact, I should thank you for pointing that out. Because I've been having trouble with a class, and was thinking about quitting. But no. I'm going to stay the course."

"What class?" Suspicion dripped from his voice.

"Doesn't matter," I said. "Point is, you've made me aware of a pattern I need to break. Thank you, big brother."

"...You're welcome."

"Oh," I said. "And I didn't quit the family business over money. It was because Uncle Charles' passing made me realize that construction isn't my path in life. Don't worry, though. I promise I won't come begging for a job, no matter how bad things get."

"Don't be stupid," Jonathan said. "You're still my brother. You know I'll help you if you need it."

"I do. And that goes both ways, big brother. And now, if you'll excuse me, I have homework to get to."

"How are classes going?"

"Not bad. Maybe better than I thought. Talk to you later."

Jonathan actually said goodbye this time, instead of just hanging up on me. And then I went downstairs to continue my visualization exercises.

Yes. I'd stick with this. Even when it got tough.

11

The months flew by. Latin was a bitch, but my newfound sense of commitment saw my grades improving in all my classes. Well, my community college classes, since my ... home studies weren't graded.

But if anything, they were going even better. The three foundational practices fed each other. I'd started imagining my route in detail before going out for my run. And while I was running, I slipped into a kind of meditation where I didn't care about the passage of time, but I was acutely aware of everything around me while I ran.

Birds, pedestrians and traffic, of course, but they were the easy part. The obvious stuff. But as I kept on, I began noticing not just the baking bread smell of the little boulangerie I passed each day, but I started noticing when they added pumpkin spice to their mix. When they were baking cupcakes instead of bread. That kind of thing.

I became aware of the rhythm of my whole neighborhood. How I could tell by the number of people and cars when the MAX was running late. How strong winds did more to cut down pedestrian traffic than rain. That sort of thing.

And I didn't realize I was becoming aware of these things. Not at first. The first time I noticed, the sequence went like this: I was coming back from my run and decided to stop by the boulangerie for one of their marionberry cupcakes.

As soon as I made that decisions, I stopped running, up close to the glass front of the laundromat, where the heat from the dryers would reach me through the window and stave off the chill of the early November wind.

I thought about why I decided to stop for cupcakes. Why today, and not yesterday or tomorrow?

The answers just came to me. I'd smelled them baking. I knew they'd be fresh. I knew the MAX was delayed because I could hear and smell the traffic from MLK, and from the way people avoiding it drove too fast down this street, heading for their alternate route.

The MAX delay would slow the boulangerie's regulars – the locals who stopped by for coffee or a snack on their way home from work, or maybe just for a loaf of fresh bread – which meant I could likely pop in, grab a cupcake to go, and still get home before the rain hit. Because from the smell and feel of the wind, I had about fifteen minutes. Plenty of time. Today.

I started laughing as I left the laundromat to see about my cupcake. I already felt like some kind of wizard. And I hadn't even gotten to the *magic* part of studying magic yet.

That sort of thing happened more and more often. In becoming more aware of my surroundings, I became more aware of my fellow students on campus. The ways they interacted. The ways they portrayed themselves, and the truths I could spot, hiding in the camouflage of their actions and gestures.

Led to my making friends with Becky. She was in my European History class. The sort of girl who's painfully shy. But I thought she was pretty, with her sparkling blue eyes and her rich brown hair.

The shyness, though, kept her hiding in the back of the class, going generally unnoticed. Until my training made me aware enough to realize that she watched me come into class every day.

So I'd started smiling at her when I came in. And after a couple of days of that, she started smiling back. A couple of classes later, she agreed to get coffee when the lecture was over. Which was when I discovered she was *much* smarter than me.

Becky was actually a high school junior – which quickly quelled any ideas I might've had about romance – who scheduled community college classes around her high school load, so she'd have more credits when it came time to go to a "real" college.

I *almost* called her on that "real" college crack, but I didn't want to risk driving her back into her shell. I was enjoying getting to know her. It was good to have someone to talk with. Someone who had no other agenda, except maybe to discuss class sometimes. Which, honestly, probably benefitted me more than her.

And once my lessons in actual magic began, it was good for me to have someone normal to talk to on a regular basis. Helped keep me grounded, while I was training myself to raise power and move it through my system.

Not my physical body, per se. No. According to my uncle's notes, everyone has multiple bodies. Physical, etheric, astral ... and a couple of others I'd apparently learn about later. And the kind of power I was raising moved through the etheric and astral bodies.

Weirdest part of that? After the first few days of practicing, I could *feel* the power when I moved it. Like the tiniest bit of pressure along my fingers and hands, then up my arms, across my shoulders, and down my other arm to my other hand.

The question I had was this: was I really feeling power move through me? Or was I imagining it, because I'd been training my visualization skills to include the sense of touch?

That was the sort of concern that would have derailed the old me. Possibly led to my quitting. But I was trying a new approach to life. So I chose to trust the process. Certainly doing so had been working for me so far. I was in the best shape of my life, my mind was clearer than ever before, and I felt more in touch with my surroundings than I'd believed possible.

Besides. Eventually Uncle Charles would *have* to give me some kind of exercise that yielded proof. Then the results would speak for themselves.

That exercise came in December. I'd been raising and moving power for weeks at that point. Connecting into the flows of the universe itself, according to Uncle Charles. And finally it had come time to put some of that power to use.

I was to pick some small desire. Nothing too big. Uncle Charles' example was a bear claw, his favorite kind of pastry. I made mine a chocolate muffin.

Next, I was to pick some small, innocuous object. Something easy to carry, that wouldn't draw attention to itself. I chose an old penny.

Finally, I had to raise power as I'd been taught, then shunt that power into the penny, and imagine my desire coming true. He called this "patterning" the power.

When I first did this, Uncle Charles wrote, *I patterned the power by imagining someone – a generic hand – giving me a bear claw. And sure enough, when I stopped by a Plaid Pantry later that morning to pick a newspaper, the clerk offered me a bear claw from the local coffee shop. Still warm in its little paper bag. "My girlfriend brought it for me," he said. "Really sweet of her, but I can't stand these things. You want it?"*

I reread the instructions three times, to make sure I didn't miss anything, then cast my spell. Or, technically, made what Uncle Charles called a one-use talisman.

When Becky and I grabbed coffee after class that day, she surprised me ... with a home-baked chocolate muffin. She called it a thank-you for being a good friend.

I know it sounds like a little nothing. Something that could be – some would say *should* be – written off as coincidence. But everything big starts with something small. And though coincidence doesn't inherently *imply* causality, coincidence doesn't exactly rule it out, either.

No. That muffin was a small thing, all right. But it was proof. All the proof I needed.

My commitment was now iron-clad.

12

LOTS OF LITTLE THINGS STARTED GOING RIGHT FOR ME AFTER THAT. THE timing of MAX train cars tended to coincide with when I'd need them. Latin and History tests tended to include the things the things I understood best (though to be fair, I studied my butt off). Stuff like that.

According to my uncle's notes, those were indications that I was getting better at living in harmony with the world around me.

It wasn't magic, per se. I wasn't casting spells for these things, or at least not anything more than the occasional single-use talisman when I expected trouble.

I have to admit, though, that some of my good luck might've been the work of local spirits. Because I'd reached a point in my studies where I'd begun making daily offerings to the spirits.

The light and heat of a candle. The smoke of a stick of incense. Small bits of raised power. Little tokens of friendship and appreciation offered to the spirits of the world around me.

Because, according to my uncle's notebooks, there were spirits of the land and spirits of the elements all around us, all the time. And more than that, every house had its spirits, every neighborhood, every city, every business...

Everything that could be thought of as a unit or collective in some way was guaranteed to have at least one spirit associated with it. And making offerings to those spirits did two things: it placated any of them I might accidentally have aggravated, and it drew positive attention from those who might've been neutral, or well-disposed towards me already.

Take the MAX for instance. I included the spirits of the MAX trains in my offerings. Now, if I'd been the type of guy to swear and curse about the MAX trains when they were late, or crowded, or messy, or who grumbled when he had to take the train at all, I might already have been on their bad side.

But that was never me. I always kind of liked taking the MAX. Felt more socially responsible than driving, and helped me feel connected to my city.

So the spirit of the MAX trains was probably pretty neutral about me, from the outset. But by the time I'd been making regular offerings, the gestalt spirit of the MAX was likely growing well-disposed towards me.

That could be important, if it ever got to the point where I needed to perform a ritual to ask the MAX trains for something. But even if not, I figured it was better to make more friends than enemies in life.

So I cast a *wide* net in my offerings.

In any event, whatever the specific cause behind my run of luck, according to the notebooks, such little niceties of life were a side effect of my training.

And I was training hard. Apart from offerings and the four foundation exercises (the fourth was raising and moving power), my daily regimen now included four rituals. Two that not only cleared out any "astral garbage" I might have accumulated while going about my day, but also strengthened my skills and my aura.

Which, by the way, is apparently not just the New Age bullshit thing I'd thought it was. Turns out the aura is a manifestation of the etheric and astral bodies, which are both larger than the physical body. Who knew?

The other two daily rituals had me drawing from the universe itself, both in the form of pure, cleansing power from the overworld, and rawer, primal power from the underworld. The rituals summoned these powers and directed them into certain inherent reservoirs in my etheric and astral bodies, developing my magical potential the way lifting weights built muscles.

I swear. A few weeks of that and I felt more *real* than I'd ever felt before. Pretty sweet, considering that the offerings and rituals *combined* didn't take more than maybe half an hour. And that was split into two sessions.

Even Mom noticed the changes in me, when I visited home for Christmas. Dad and Jonathan, not so much, but at least neither one of them yelled at me, or even loomed in unspoken anger. Made me wonder if Jonathan had gotten Dad to back off, after our last big conversation.

Anyway, Mom, of course, was convinced that the changes she saw were proof I had a new girl in my life. But honestly, I hadn't done much dating. Not exactly a threat to my uncle's no-overnight-guests-for-six-months rule.

In fact, I only realized the six months had passed because of a surprise phone call from Mr. McDonnell.

The call came while I was in the kitchen, snacking on carrot sticks and conjugating the passive paraphrastic as I prepared for my Latin final. I liked doing schoolwork at the kitchen table, and leaving the rest of the house for everything else.

I even kept my laptop – the one I brought with me from home – in a kitchen cabinet. Figured that was safer until I understood more about why my uncle kept so little computing power around him.

More than a little surprised to see McDonnell and Associates come up on the caller ID when my phone rang, I answered quickly. Mr. McDonnell sounded pleased about something. Positively avuncular.

"Charlie! Just wanted to call and let you know you're now officially clear to let your girlfriends sleep over, if you like."

I laughed. "I'll get right on that."

"I'll bet you will. How are you coming along?"

"Ah, Mr. McDonnell, I am thriving," I said with a smile.

"Glad to hear it. Glad to hear it. Money can be a positive boon, can it not?"

"It certainly opens doors," I said. "I realized the other night that I could get season tickets for the Blazers if I wanted. Really good ones. And my bank account wouldn't even notice."

"You should do it," he said, and I could hear the smile in his voice. "I think they're likely to go all the way this year. Though remember. Don't flaunt your wealth in front of your family."

"That's why I'm still driving my old Subaru," I said.

"Glad to hear it. Glad to hear it. Your uncle always said you were a smart boy."

"And now some of my grades are even proving it. Which should be borne out soon in finals."

"Still taking your college classes then. Good. Good. Education will serve you well, no matter what you want to do in life. Speaking of which, I've been wondering. Do you think you'll want to go treasure hunting? The way your uncle did?"

I felt a frisson of foreboding I couldn't explain. Something subtle had changed in Mr. McDonnell's voice. At least, I *thought* that was what it was. I wasn't sure, though. And I couldn't put my finger on *what* had changed.

Was he actually asking about treasure hunting? Or was he asking if I was studying my uncle's magic? And if so, why the roundabout approach?

Or was he waiting for *me* to broach that subject? Maybe to ask him more questions?

Either way, something definitely felt off.

I tried not to let my voice sound any different when I answered.

"I don't think I share all my uncle's interests," I said, which was true enough. That crystal skull thing, a prominent example. "For example, I'm not sure *treasure hunting* is my life's calling. But maybe I'll feel differently when I go through more of his documentaries. I plan on bingeing a bunch of them over break."

"Quite understandable," Mr. McDonnell said. His voice tried for pure reassurance, but unless I was imagining things, I thought I heard a touch of eagerness. "He certainly wanted to give you the opportunity to follow in his footsteps. But I doubt he really expected you to do so."

"Let's just say I'm still considering my options."

"Well, then I should let you know that if you'd like to part with the ... *rarer* parts of your uncle's library, I'd be happy to broker the deals for you."

"Oh?"

"Oh, certainly. Certainly. Won't even take a percentage. Wouldn't hear of it. Least I can do for Charles. And trust me, my boy. Certain of those titles will fetch a sum that even *your* bank account will notice."

"I don't know," I said carefully. "We're talking about my uncle's legacy here. It'd feel like a shame to part with it."

"Nonsense," he all but chortled. "Your uncle didn't believe in collecting for collecting's sake. He'd want those books going into the hands of those who'd appreciate them." More smile in his voice when he added, "Not to say he wouldn't want you profiting handsomely from the sale."

"I'll ... keep that in mind," I said.

"Oh, and while you're considering such things," he said, and I got that sense of apprehension again. "I believe your uncle was off researching his next treasure hunt when he passed. If he followed his usual procedures, he likely left most of his notes at home. Have you seen anything like that?"

"Yes," I said. "A great deal of notes and maps."

"Oh, and the maps too. Wonderful. Wonderful."

"What about them?"

"Well. Though your uncle always eschewed publicity, the treasure hunter community is not large, and his success was not unheard of. Whatever treasure he was tracking down, given his ... considerable talents ... it's safe to say the secret to unearthing it lies in those notes and maps."

"Yes, I suppose it must."

"Well, if you could be persuaded to part with those notes and maps, I'm sure I could fetch you quite a price for them. It's well known that Charles Warren didn't chase small treasures."

"I could see that."

"Mind you, I *would* want a commission for *this* sale. But I promise, it would be small." He laughed a low, booming laugh. "But even a small commission could amount to quite a bit, in this case."

"I guess so."

"You sound hesitant, Charlie. Why?"

"Well, we *are* talking about parting with things my uncle left me."

"Yes, it's true. And I know that you grieve for him even more than I do. But the money was only ever half the point of treasure hunting for Charles. He wanted to see those treasures back in the world, being appreciated."

"Yes, I suppose he did," I lied. Drew a deep breath. "It's a lot to think about, Mr. McDonnell. But I'll consider it."

"Wouldn't want to rush you, my boy. Last thing I'd want to do. But I must admit that the price will be higher now than it would be in a year. The fever for such things does tend to cool with time. As does confidence in their value."

"Do you know what he was after?"

"Well, no. Of course not. Your uncle never discussed what he was after until he had it in his hand. Just in case someone else got to it first."

That brought a wistful smile to my face. "That does sound like him." Another deep breath. "I'll think about it. Now if you'll excuse me, I've got tea water boiling on the stove."

I didn't. But I wanted to get off the phone.

"Best see about that then. We'll talk soon, Charlie."

He hung up, and I sat there, thinking about what I'd just been told.

Mr. McDonnell was either wrong or lying about Uncle Charles' motives for treasure hunting. If my uncle cared so much about getting lost treasures back in circulation, there wouldn't be a bunch of them in the garage, waiting to be sold.

And if Mr. McDonnell didn't know what Uncle Charles was after, how did he know the maps and notes would fetch a high price "in this case?"

What was really going on here?

13

———

THAT CALL FROM MR. MCDONNELL UPSET ME. I DON'T MEAN IT MADE me angry, either. I mean upset the way a canoe could be upset. I was thrown off-kilter. Couldn't taste my carrot sticks, not even the lingering slivers caught between my teeth. Couldn't focus on the rest of my homework, because my mind kept picking at his words. His tone. Wondering what the real meaning of the phone call had been.

I felt sure Mr. McDonnell had been after something. Maybe one or more of the grimoires? Maybe my uncle's notes and maps about that supposed shipment of orichalcum bound from Atlantis to Athens?

Plus, it was obvious that Mr. McDonnell knew something about magic. He'd been expecting me to have strange questions. He'd known...

...he'd known about familiars.

I still didn't know what familiars were yet. Hadn't gotten that far into my uncle's lesson plan. I mean, I figured familiars had to be spirits, but even that was guesswork.

Mr. McDonnell, though, he clearly knew more. He was the one who'd told me about them in the first place. Or at least, told me that

Uncle Charles had one that should've been waiting in his magic workroom, if my uncle were still alive.

What was it he'd said? Oh, yes. That the familiar would've recognized me, and allowed me access.

Did that imply that it wouldn't have allowed Mr. McDonnell access?

Was that it? He'd had the keys to my uncle's house. So, in theory, he could've come in here on his own and just taken stuff he'd wanted. Not like I'd've known any grimoires were missing. Or any maps and notes. But he sounded as though he didn't even know about all the stuff stored in the garage...

Then it hit me. Words Uncle Charles had written about the garage. In that letter I'd long since memorized from rereading.

All sorts of goodies in the garage. Some of which are protected in ways you wouldn't understand yet.

Select crates and boxes in the garage. Protected somehow. And unlike the familiar, it sounded as though these protections would survive my uncle's death.

Which means maybe there were more protections around me than I knew?

My chair legs scraped the linoleum as I pushed back from the kitchen table.

I knew what power felt like. I'd been raising, moving and directing it for months. But I'd never really gone looking for it in the wild. Just never occurred to me to do so.

Maybe it was time I started.

But first I had to get hold of myself. I shook out my hands. Rolled my neck and shoulders. Scrunched my face muscles around, then consciously relaxed them. My scalp and neck came next. Then shoulders, arms, wrists, hands, fingers. Then torso and belly, hips and pelvis, legs, knees, feet, toes.

Another deep breath and I cleared my mind. Sank into meditation for a few minutes, without keeping track how long.

Eventually I opened my eyes and stood. The late afternoon

sunlight gave my kitchen a timeless look. More like a photograph than a real place. I focused on the feel of air on my skin, even around my tee shirt and jeans and socks. Felt the nondescript warmth of that timeless sunlight.

I stretched out beyond my physical body then. Tried to feel with my etheric and astral bodies. Not searching for anything. Not yet. Just getting a sense of how my kitchen felt, so that I had something to contrast with.

I walked into the living room. Stood still, breathing slowly and deeply, trying to judge how this room felt different.

A little cooler, without the afternoon sun exposure. But if there was any other change, I couldn't feel it. Bedroom, bathroom, map room, all the same. Warmed by the central heating, but otherwise not drawing my attention.

I went to the front door. Reached for the knob.

Something.

Along the door and the walls. Power had been channeled into something here. Given a pattern of some sort, though I didn't know how to read it. Could tell it was there, but not any details. At least I knew this power wasn't dangerous to *me*, because I came and went through this door every day. More or less.

So I opened the door and stepped through.

It was like stepping through a waterfall's ghost. Power tested me, and allowed me to pass unhindered. Whatever pattern was here, I was part of it. Accepted by it.

Protected in ways you wouldn't understand yet.

This was the kind of thing Uncle Charles was talking about, wasn't he? Protection spells. And he'd left one on the house.

What else had he left?

I took a moment to get a feel of outside, on my front porch. And not just the winter air, which was too cold to be outside in just jeans and a tee shirt – not to mention freezing concrete under my stocking feet. I wouldn't be outside long, though. I pretended to go check my mailbox, as an excuse to go to the sidewalk.

Another barrier at the sidewalk. This one ... softer. Porous, maybe. But I didn't know if that meant weaker, or just that it was more forgiving, or something else entirely. I just know that I felt less here, passing through onto the sidewalk, than I'd felt passing through the front door. More like a sprinkler's ghost than a waterfall's.

Geez, how had I been living inside two protection spells all this time without suspecting a thing? I had *so much* to learn.

Well, I had lost time to make up for. So I walked the rest of the grounds in that awareness-meditation state. Learned that the kitchen entrance had the same kind of feel as the front door. So did the garage, for that matter. Meaning it had a protection spell of its own, but it also had smaller spells protecting more than a dozen crates and boxes inside the garage. And those were just the ones I could find that day.

I discovered yet another spell of some kind at the entrance to the basement. But no others past that. At least, nothing I noticed.

Well. So was that my answer? Mr. McDonnell had to deal with me because he couldn't get past my uncle's spells?

What was I thinking? The man was a lawyer. And at least *seemed* to be Uncle Charles' friend. I had no right to suspect him of wrongdoing. Not just because he wanted to help me sell books, maps and notes he thought I wouldn't use.

Yes, he'd sounded eager. But he might've been eager for a chance to buy one or more of those grimoires, since apparently they're quite rare. And maybe the commission he'd make helping me sell the notes and maps would be enough to set him up for a luxurious retirement or something.

No reason to suspect him of anything more than that.

What was the big deal about orichalcum anyway? Even the ancient Romans didn't consider it more valuable than gold. At least, according what the internet.

On the other hand, it *was* supposed to be associated with Atlantis. So maybe finding this shipment would also find proof that Atlantis was real? And maybe clues about where it actually was?

I needed to know more about orichalcum. More than quick internet searches could tell me.

But first, I *had* to finish studying for my Latin final. After all, *tempus fugit.*

14

I MADE MY ORICHALCUM RESEARCH WAIT UNTIL I WAS NOT ONLY DONE studying, but had performed my evening rituals and eaten my dinner. Stir-fried chicken with broccoli, cauliflower and bell peppers, both red and green.

I carried a glass of Diet Eruption Cola in the map room, and started reviewing what Uncle Charles had left there. Sought out his coded, handwritten crip notes on the maps, as well as reading over the many pages of actual notepaper he'd left lying around. I was getting so good at his cipher now that I could read and write it as fast as I did English. Or rather, as fast I could the Latinate letters I'd grown up with. Because no matter what the characters were, the words, grammar and syntax were still English.

The notes and maps in that room weren't all that much help, though. They seemed to focus on the shipment he was looking for, rather than the metal itself.

I went through every disc, every tape, and even every roll of film I could find in the living room, but I couldn't find a single documentary about orichalcum. So I had to settle for watching the ones about Atlantis.

Four freaking documentaries. More than five-and-a-half hours of viewing. Care to guess how many references to orichalcum I found? Three. And the sum total of information those references contained was that the metal was supposedly mined in Atlantis, and that at some point the mines ran dry.

It was after midnight now, so I went to bed. Frustrated.

The next day, eager as I was to get back at it, I forced myself to get up and follow my routines. Morning meditation and rituals before going for my run, then showering, breakfasting, and off to school to take my Latin final. Last final of the semester.

By the time I got home from class, I had an idea. I'd gone through the documentaries, yes, but Uncle Charles' downstairs library had plenty of books about the kinds of weird things he had on video.

Surely one of them would have the answer.

Surely not, as it turned out.

Hours I spent looking, but I found no books about orichalcum down there. I did find references to the metal in his three books about Atlantis, but they amounted to the same information I'd gotten from the documentaries. In other words, useless.

Frustration began to well up, so I cleared my head through a few belly breaths. The books weren't useless. Neither were those documentaries. Surely they had something to say about Atlantis that made them worth keeping, or Uncle Charles would've dumped them ages ago.

So they weren't useless. Even if they were no help, in this instance.

The answers had to be here somewhere. Given the notes and maps Uncle Charles left behind when he went sailing, I simply couldn't believe he'd've brought all his research about the *metal itself* with him. Couldn't see how it would be useful. I went down to slip where the sailboat waited and searched it, even the hidden safe mentioned in that first notebook. (The safe was empty save for a not-insubstantial amount of cash in a few different currencies.)

Which meant the answer *had* to be here. Somewhere.

But if Uncle Charles had any research I hadn't found, those secrets weren't in the map room, the living room, or the main library.

I flirted with the idea of checking the grimoires, but shelved that for a last resort. I hadn't gotten to read any of those as part of my studies yet, and I figured I should trust Uncle Charles' judgment there. Save those books until he said I was ready for them.

But the answers had to be *someplace*...

Wait! What about the *garage*?

Of course!

I went into my uncle's – well now *my* – magic workroom and picked up the first notebook again. I flipped past the key to his cipher for the garage catalog.

"Hah!" I cried, pumping a fist in triumph.

Second row, right-hand side, fourth column, third from the top. *Orichalcum Research*.

I put the notebook back and sped off on my mission.

This box turned out to be one of those under some kind of protection spell.

"It's me, Uncle Charles," I muttered. "I swear."

I stretched up onto my toes, reached out and touched the box.

No reaction.

Figuring that was good, I went for the lifter and ladder, bringing them both where I needed them. I didn't know how Uncle Charles would have gotten that box down, but I hoisted the lifter's arms to the level of the two boxes I needed to remove. Then I climbed the rolling ladder and stacked all three boxes on the lifter's arms.

I climbed back down. Lowered the lifter's arms. Set the box I wanted aside, restacked the first two in proper order, and used the lifter to put them back.

Tempted as I was to open my prize and examine the contents here, that didn't feel like the right move. Plus, it was freaking freezing out here! I mean, the garage was insulated, but that only helped so much during a Portland winter.

Also, and maybe this was paranoia on my part, but I still got a funny feeling, every time I thought about those small shifts in Mr. McDonnell's manner. Made me feel that extra precautions might be in order.

I brought the box back into the house, then down the stairs and all the way to the desk in the magic workroom. It occurred to me then that this downstairs area should've felt colder than it did. The central heat didn't get down here, and it was all concrete. I mean, it was *cool* down here, but the temp outside wasn't far above freezing...

Question for another time.

I sat on the roller chair under the track lighting, and set the box on the desk. Wasn't that heavy, now that I thought about it. Not as heavy as it would've been, had it been stuffed with paper or weightier things.

I just hoped whatever was inside would be enough.

My heart was pounding as I reached for the lid. No folding top for this one. A separate lid that lifted off.

With my senses on high alert, the moment I touched the lid, I felt a tingle in my fingers from its protective magics. But as I lifted the lid, the tingling dispersed.

Had I just broken the protective spell?

Crap! I didn't know how to put it back!

I shook my head. Rolled my shoulders. Took another belly breath. Done was done. Worse came to worse, I could keep the box down here somewhere. In the torchiere lamp room maybe. That would at least keep it behind two locks and three protection spells. Ought to be plenty.

I set the box lid aside and took a look at what that spell had been protecting.

Big shock. A series of manila folders. Guess maybe I'd been hoping for a sample of the metal or something like that. Maybe a book. Preferably full of annotated bookmarks, just in case I was the one going through these files, and not my uncle.

No luck there.

Each of the manila folders were filled with handwritten notes. No articles. No letters from acquaintances. No printouts or photocopies. No newspaper or magazine articles. Just handwritten notes, all done in Uncle Charles' cipher.

Then I thought to look at the manila folders themselves, and saw that each was labeled, though for a moment I thought I was getting his cipher wrong, because the lettering didn't make sense. But then on the seventh I saw the word "Vatican" and everything else clicked into place.

MSS wasn't a misinterpretation on my part. It had to mean manuscript. So the seventh was "Vatican Manuscript 6321" Presumably the six thousand, three hundred twenty-first manuscript logged into the Vatican's private library.

Uncle Charles had gotten personal access to the Vatican's private library? Whoa! I mean, if anything, our family was Lutheran. Figure we'd be the *last* people the *Vatican* would allow into their literary holiest of holies.

Just how good were Uncle Charles' contacts?

Anyway, eight of the manila folders were full of notes taken from manuscripts at the Vatican. Four more from the British Museum. One from the archives of the Library of Congress. But the first six? The ones that had thrown me?

Those didn't have place names. They had private names. Names like Kovacs, Mathers, Scott, Donaldson, Frost, and Von Behren. So these manuscripts had to be part of these people's private collections.

I wondered a moment how Uncle Charles had gotten those people to let him read their treasures. Had he paid them? Maybe in money or magic? Or were these friends of his I'd never heard about?

Friends who might never learn of his passing, because I didn't know to tell them...

15

———————

I set aside my research for a moment. Went upstairs into the kitchen, which was where my phone's signal was strongest. Called Mr. McDonnell.

"Charlie! Glad you called. Shall I begin putting out feelers regarding those maps and notes? Or perhaps the grimoires?"

"Not yet, Mr. McDonnell. I was just curious about something. Did my uncle have a friend named Kovacs?"

"Kovacs … Kovacs…" Mr. McDonnell said, and I could hear the thoughtful frown on his face. "Yes. I remember now. There was a Kovacs among the list of those I needed to notify of his passing. M. Kovacs. I remember thinking it was odd that no first name was listed, and the address was only a mailbox in Denmark. Why do you ask?"

"Just ran across the name while digging through his stuff. Worried that it might've been a friend who hadn't heard the bad news."

"Well, thank you for bringing it to my attention, but I can assure you that I've notified everyone your uncle wanted notified. Including M. Kovacs."

"Good," I said, relieved.

"Charlie," Mr. McDonnell said, avuncular chiding in his voice now, "you weren't thinking of going around me to sell those notes or grimoires were you?"

"No, Mr. McDonnell. Definitely not."

"Good. Because I can guarantee you that I'll get you the best price. I've done this kind of thing before, and not just for your uncle."

"Oh?"

"Of course! As I told you, the community of elite treasure hunters is not large. I keep in touch with all the major players, and have done legal work for several. They know me to be a trusted source."

"Oh, I thought you were talking about the grimoires," I lied.

"No, no," he said, chuckling. "Your uncle always did his own business on that front. But the antiquarian book market is ... rarified territory, Charlie. Especially when it comes to collectors of true occult masterworks, such as the books in your uncle's collection. Believe me when I say that going to someplace like Sotheby's or Christie's would net you chump change compared to what a private auction could do among the right people."

"And you know the right people?"

"I do. Among both the top occultists and treasure hunters. There is no one better positioned to get you maximum value for either your uncle's grimoires or his research than I am."

"I'll keep that in mind."

"Charlie, you really ought to do more than that," Mr. McDonnell said, and from the weariness in his voice, I began to think his patience was thinning. "I know, I know. These were your uncle's possessions, and you have trouble bringing yourself to part with them. Especially since you're wealthy enough that you don't believe you need the money. And maybe you don't. But there are other considerations."

"Really? Because you have to admit, you've been pushing the money angle pretty hard."

"I have, and for good reason. Wealth *does* matter in this world, Charlie. No matter what you wish to do in life, be it seeking out luxuries and joys, helping others, or what have you. All things are made possible by money. And the truth is, the more you have, the more you can do."

"But how much does one person need?"

"An immaterial question," Mr. McDonnell said firmly. "You have that wealth *right now*. It's already in your possession. Those grimoires represent a material form of wealth. Those notes and maps – your uncle's research – represent a more ephemeral form of wealth. The manifest value of his expertise and time. Are you following me so far?"

"Yes," I said, trying not to feel insulted by the question.

"Now, I freely admit that the grimoires are a safe investment, in that their value could be considered evergreen. By which I mean they might not *increase* in value, but they will not appreciably *decrease* in value either. Apart, of course, from minor fluctuations representing the latest trends and fads, which even scholars and practitioners are not immune to."

"I could see that," I said carefully.

"Your uncle's notes and maps, though, are different. They represent a *perishable* investment, in that their value will inevitably peak, then decline with time."

"How so?"

"News of your uncle's death has had just over six months to spread through the upper tier of the treasure hunter community. Given his reputation, his peers' *second* thought on hearing of his passing – second to their personal reaction to the news, of course – must be to wonder what he was working on, and whether or not they could complete what he started. For as I've told you before, your uncle did not chase small treasures."

"I remember," I said.

"Good. Now. The first instincts among those peers would be to try to figure out for themselves what he was doing. But your uncle was always too clever for that. Too cautious. Won't take them long to realize he was working in secret again. And that will only build their zeal, for they will imagine his last project to be his greatest."

"And you're saying that zeal will fade?"

"Inevitably. They will become distracted by some new discovery or opportunity. And more than that, with time, the strength of even your uncle's reputation will fade in their minds. They'll begin to imagine themselves his equal. Perhaps even his better. They'll imagine that his death represented not the magnificence of the treasure he sought, but a failure on his part. Proof of imagined feet of clay, if you will."

"So to maximize the value—"

"No," Mr. McDonnell said firmly. "You *cannot control* their value. That is a large part of my point, Charlie, so I do hope you're listening to me. You are in possession of an investment that is near the peak of its value. Continue to hold it while you dither, and you will soon begin throwing away money you cannot recover. To *no one's* benefit."

"Okay," I said slowly. "I could see that."

"Shall I begin sending out feelers then?"

"Wait," I said. "You said something about other considerations?"

"Well the other considerations are things I've mentioned before, Charlie. Charles Warren never believed in collecting for collecting's sake. He either put his possessions to use, or he passed them along to those that would." I could hear the smile in his voice as he continued, "Usually profiting in the bargain, of course, but that was to be expected."

"And you're saying I should follow his example."

"I do believe it's what Charles would've wanted. Really. Why leave a portion of your wealth tied up in books whose value increases only commensurate with inflation? Why not sell them, and invest that money someplace that will pay you greater dividends, while ensuring that they're put to their intended use?"

"What if I'm not sure I want to get rid of them yet?"

"Then by all means, hold onto them until you're certain, Charlie. There's no urgency on that front."

"But there is on the maps and notes. Because their value is perishable."

"It *is*," Mr. McDonnell said, "but in this case the loss is not only to your own bottom line. The world loses as well."

"How so?"

"Right now the zeal is at its zenith. Your uncle's peers would *fight* to be the one to complete his final work and present it to the world. But as time passes, so does their urgency. The memory of your uncle's brilliance will fade. They will not only *pay* less for those notes and maps, they'll *expect* less from what they purchase. Instead to throwing themselves into your uncle's final project, they'll pick at it over time. Question it. They might never complete it at all."

He sighed heavily. "And that, Charlie, would be the biggest shame of all. And a great loss to all humanity."

"But how do you know that? You said you don't know what he was working on."

"I knew your uncle well, Charlie. Well indeed. Well enough to know that he was working on something for which the world itself waits with bated breath."

"I can't decide that right now."

"I understand, Charlie. But do decide soon. Not just for yourself, but for the world."

I thanked him and got off the phone.

Mr. McDonnell had told me exactly what I wanted to hear. So why did I get that nagging feeling again, that something was wrong? That he was hiding something from me?

And if so, what could it be?

16

THAT FEELING THAT SOMETHING WAS WRONG KEPT NAGGING AT ME, AS I sat there at the kitchen table, thinking over that conversation while rain pounded the world outside my windows.

What was it about my dealings with Mr. McDonnell that left me feeling ... unsafe? That he had an agenda beyond what he was telling me?

If it was just about money, that would be one thing. I had more money now than I knew what to do with. Especially since I couldn't get flashy with it anytime soon.

Heck, I hadn't even bought those Blazers' season tickets yet.

No, I wouldn't begrudge Mr. McDonnell a cut of the sale of those maps and notes. Or a cut of the sale of ... well, that one was moot. I had no intention of selling the grimoires. But the maps and notes about that orichalcum shipment, though. I didn't really have a persuasive reason not to sell those. I had plenty of keepsakes from my uncle to count as his legacy.

But what if Mr. McDonnell's agenda was something else?

He knew something about what my uncle was looking for. I was sure of that. That one slip he'd made about the value "in this case." He hadn't meant because it was Uncle Charles' final project. He'd meant something else.

Which meant he *knew* something else.

Which meant maybe that real orichalcum – if it existed – was a big deal...

I had to do two things. I had to go through those notes. See what the fuss – if anything – was about this orichalcum. And I had to find some way to contact this M. Kovacs. Or maybe one of the others. Frost. Mathers. Whoever.

My uncle had had other friends. People who knew what he was really about. People who weren't Mr. McDonnell.

I needed to get in touch with one of them. Hear someone else's perspective.

Alas, though, I didn't know where to start with those six surnames I'd found on those manila folders. I didn't even know the address of that mailbox in Denmark belonging to M. Kovacs. So for now I had no way to contact any of them.

Orichalcum first then.

I went back down to the magic workroom and dug into those manila folders with renewed purpose.

I was at it late into the night. I took breaks only for my evening rituals and meditation. Well, and dinner. Man does not live on ritual alone. But I ordered delivery, rather than cooking, to save time. Grilled salmon with mixed vegetables and Diet Eruption Cola.

My uncle's notes broke down into two categories: transcriptions of passages from those manuscripts – presumably verbatim – and his personal notes about what those passages meant, within some wider context. His personal notes were at the end of each manila folder, following the current transcription, so in each case I read the transcriptions first, then my uncle's commentary about what he'd learned from that manuscript.

I don't mind admitting, it was tough sledding for quite a while there. I was determined to read the transcriptions first, so I didn't miss anything. And their language was *archaic*.

And I don't just mean the handful of them written in English. Most of these manuscripts were in Latin. Some of it classical Latin, some of it church Latin, some of it ... I'm not sure. Languages evolved with time. In Latin's case that seemed to still be true, even after its time as a daily use language had faded into memory. Its survival in scholarly circles had seen to it that the language continued to grow and evolve, albeit slower than other, "living" languages.

What that part meant was that I needed to go upstairs and fetch my Latin textbooks and dictionaries.

I actually owed Dad a little thanks there. He insisted that when I started learning a language, I go out and buy two or three dictionaries. Good ones, not cheap ones. A translation dictionary, as in English-to-X and X-to-English. A recent dictionary of the other language. And, if I could get it, an *old* dictionary of the other language. He said that the older dictionaries always had lost and forgotten words, and exemplified the etymology of a language in ways that the newer dictionaries often eschewed.

Yes. That was all from *Dad*. I sometimes thought he should've been a linguist. He spoke four languages that I knew of, and always seemed to be picking at more.

So I had excellent Latin resources available, without having to resort to my phone and the internet. Good thing, because even with all that on my side, I still wasn't sure I was reading the Latin right. I mean, the way the manuscript writers handled grammar and structure seemed to *imply* so much. And I hadn't been at the language all that long.

So really, by the end of that first night's work, I had a decent idea of what the first manuscript transcription said, but not much more than that.

If I was right, though, then orichalcum might be a very big deal indeed.

In this case, Uncle Charles' notes at the end of that folder weren't much help. They were little more than excited commentary about the potential of orichalcum, if any of the real stuff could be found.

Unfortunately, those notes didn't go into detail about what that potential might be. Because, apparently, *he* understood the Latin quite well. Which meant I was afraid to speculate, in case I was wrong.

Also, this was only the first folder of *nineteen*. Way too soon for conclusions.

After that first night, I was able to go through about two folders a day. Doing my best to translate from Latin where necessary, which meant almost all of them. And honestly, the ones that were in "English" weren't much better. The spellings. The syntax. Hardly recognizable as the language I used every day.

And the notes Uncle Charles left at the end of each folder didn't help with the translations. It seemed that *he* understood every freaking word and implication. So these notes were really his running commentary about possibilities and likelihoods. Which sources he considered more trustworthy and why. Reminders to cross-reference ideas with other books or manuscripts, but even those were little more than shorthand.

I felt like a grade schooler trying to read someone's doctoral research.

So the better part of two weeks went by before I got to the twentieth folder.

Yes. The twentieth. I know I'd said nineteen earlier. But that was because I'd counted the ones labeled by manuscript, and not thought about the unlabeled folder at the back.

That was the folder with Uncle Charles' final notes and thoughts, his interpretations, and, I was pretty sure, the results of his cross-referencing with other research.

And it was this folder that really brought together the mishmash of half-gleaned notions in my head, and filtered them down to three important points.

First, Atlantis was real. It may have been an island, rather than a continent, but it was a real place. A physical land mass in the Atlantic Ocean, somewhere westish of Greece.

Or at the very least, Uncle Charles seemed convinced that this was true. And some things he'd read in those nineteen manuscripts – things that had clearly gone over *my* head, because I hadn't picked them up – confirmed for him information he'd learned from other sources.

Something to do with an oblique reference to changes in tides and currents. But if I wanted to know more, I'd have to go back to the catalog to find Uncle Charles' Atlantis research. And far as I was concerned, that could wait.

Second, the island or continent of Atlantis had once possessed and traded a metal unique to their shores: orichalcum. The references different writers had made in those manuscripts indicated personal experience with small quantities of the metal in their own experiments. And their reports about the metal – as well as their purposes in attaining and employing it – had been too similar in *almost* all cases.

There were discrepancies. Some small, some large. The small ones didn't seem to trouble Uncle Charles. He wrote them off as "expected," from a series of writers with differing levels of "skill, talent and knowledge."

The larger discrepancies apparently troubled Uncle Charles even less. He concluded that they were either blinds – lies told to deceive the uninitiated, but that the knowledgeable would see right through – or simply false. Indications that the writer had never gotten their hands on "real" orichalcum in the first place.

Which leads to...

Third. What orichalcum was.

It was a metal, all right. Could be worked like metal, with a hardness that made it not entirely useless in armor. Its hue was somewhere between gold and copper, and had even been used in coins at some point. So far, nothing more than the common details mentioned in the books and documentaries I'd already been through. The kind of stuff probably easily found online.

But there was more.

The Atlanteans had lied when they told people they'd mined it. It was closer to a star metal. Something that had fallen out of the sky, and was not otherwise to be found on earth. Which was why no other orichalcum mines had been found anywhere in the world.

But it hadn't fallen from the *sky*, as the Atlanteans had initially thought. It had fallen from Olympus.

According to the notes and research in this box, orichalcum was a calcified form of ambrosia. The food of the Greek and Roman (and possibly Atlantean) gods.

Consuming true ambrosia was said to grant the *immortality* of the gods.

Consuming orichalcum alas, proved fatal, according to reports.

However.

These manuscripts held recipes for purifying the orichalcum. Transforming it back into ambrosia.

A literal recipe for immortality.

When I realized that, I just sat there at the desk for a long, long time.

17

———

Immortality. That's what Uncle Charles had been chasing when he died.

Ironic, in a way. Or at least poetic.

Immortality. Just a few months ago, the mere concept would've been ludicrous to me. Literally the stuff of myths.

But I was already seeing – and feeling – results from my study of magic. Small results, yes, but results nonetheless. What I didn't have was a calibration about the *upper* limit of what was possible.

What I did know was that my uncle, who'd turned away from the family business, had managed to accumulate a significant fortune without drawing attention to himself. As a treasure hunter, yet.

If *that* didn't constitute proof that magic could accomplish quite a bit, I wasn't sure what would.

Immortality, though. It still sounded outrageous. Beyond the pale. Like conjuring gold out of thin air. The kind of fantasy stuff he'd said wasn't possible.

And yet...

And yet Uncle Charles had made clear that he'd discovered a *number* of truths that had fallen between the cracks of what people commonly knew and accepted as real. I'd only scratched the surface with my study of magic.

That garage held a lot more research than it did treasure. No telling just how many weird truths my uncle had found that I *never* would've guessed.

Maybe bigfoot. Maybe aliens. Maybe vampires.

Maybe immortality.

Wait. I was getting ahead of myself.

What did it matter if immortality was real? It *might* be. *If* any of those formulae worked, and could turn orichalcum into ambrosia.

I didn't even *want* to get into the possible theological implications of all this. No, I had to focus on what I'd learned, and what it meant. Here. In *this* world.

Uncle Charles probably had multiple goals on his last hunt, with each leading to the next. Finding the orichalcum shipment would've provided tangible proof that that Atlantis had existed, and that orichalcum was more than just an alloy used later by the Romans.

Next, he'd've tested those formulae. Tried to purify some of the orichalcum into ambrosia, proving that *ambrosia* was real too.

Of course, part of the proof there would mean sampling the ambrosia. And becoming immortal, in the bargain.

Probably his ideal endgame. If only because who could resist the chance to taste the literal food of the gods?

I didn't know whether or not I wanted to be immortal. But I wasn't sure *I* could say no, if someone offered me a taste of real ambrosia. How do you turn that down, and not wonder for the rest of your life what it would've tasted like?

What was it Uncle Charles used to say? Oh, yes. "We'll build that bridge when we need to cross it."

So how much of all this did Mr. McDonnell know? Because he definitely knew more than he was letting on. Easy to believe that he was after more than a cut of the proceeds from selling those maps and notes.

Oh, hell. That wasn't something I could guess. For all I knew, he might've known nothing and just wanted a nice payday, or he might've known everything and been chasing immortality himself.

The real question was, what should I do about it?

Uncle Charles, he seemed to have been on the verge of a major discovery when he vanished. I mean, according to those transcriptions, if *any* of those formulae had been even *close* to accurate, they only needed a few ounces of orichalcum to work on. But that shipment had included "fifty talents" worth.

That sounded like a lot.

But how much was it?

I shook myself out of my reverie. I'd been sitting here in the cool basement too long. My knees even popped when I stood, and a couple of my toes had gone to sleep. My stomach growled. When had I last eaten? That peanut butter sandwich around noon?

I went upstairs.

My bedroom was dark. Streetlights leaked in through cracks in the curtains. The heat was running, but the room was already warmer than downstairs. But then, I'd taken to wearing sweatshirts and good slippers when I went down to work, and today was no exception.

My phone peeped at me, complaining that hours' worth of notifications had to come through all at once. A couple of text messages from Becky. Email notifications about things that seemed shockingly mundane.

A missed call from Mr. McDonnell. He'd left a voicemail.

Odd, that such a little thing could tighten up my shoulders. Make my heart beat heavier. I didn't like that. So I tossed the phone onto my bed, went back downstairs and performed my evening meditations and rituals.

With my head clear once more, I went back up to my bedroom and flipped on the light switch. This was the room most changed since I moved in. More bookshelves for my books, and a stack of boxes for other possessions I hadn't gotten around to unpacking.

I checked my phone notifications again, and felt steadier about them.

Becky's texts weren't urgent. Just chatty stuff and an invitation to lunch at a food cart she loved for its Mediterranean wraps. I accepted the invitation, and sent her a joke about having become trapped on a Latin peak and being unable to decline my way to safer ground.

The emails I ignored for now.

I played the voicemail.

"Charlie! Hope I'm not intruding on winter festivities. Hate to do a thing like that. Especially since I'm sure a healthy young man such as yourself is enjoying the many fine diversions wealth can provide in our fair city."

He chortled before continuing.

"I don't want to rush you, but the clock is ticking on the value of those notes and maps. I do hope you're giving serious consideration to letting me sell them for you. If it helps, think of the sale as one last gift from your uncle to the world. The fruits of one more hunt. Even if he isn't the one who completes it, it would be his work that made it possible.

"I think this is what Charles would want.

"So please, get back to me soon. Just say the word, and I'll send a courier to pick up the notes and maps and get the process started. Safe to say I'll be able to get you a tidy sum, and it shouldn't take me more than a month to complete the transaction. Should make for a very happy new year for everyone.

"And I know the grimoires feel like a personal matter to Charles, but remember, he kept them for utility, not sentiment. If you won't use them, I'm sure he'd rather see them sold than moldering away on your shelves.

"And though they won't fetch anything close to what those notes and maps will bring, those grimoires do represent something of windfall unto themselves.

"Think it over, Charlie, and get back to me soon. Goodbye."

Wow. A lot to unpack there.

First, whatever else I'd managed, I'd convinced Mr. McDonnell I wasn't taking up my uncle's magic. That felt like a small victory unto itself.

Taking up the practice of magic, according to my uncle, meant asserting four traits: knowledge, daring, will, and silence. In hiding my practice from the only person in a position to suspect it, I felt I was embracing that fourth trait.

And I had the feeling it would reap some benefits.

Second, he didn't just want to sell those maps and notes for me. Mr. McDonnell wanted them *in his hands* while looking for a buyer. That suggested that he definitely had plans beyond just selling them. Maybe he wanted a partnership. Maybe he wanted to evaluate them himself.

Whatever. I was convinced now that he wasn't offering to broker this "sale" for me or for Uncle Charles. He wanted something for himself in this, beyond an infusion of cash.

Heck, I wasn't even sure Uncle Charles would *want* anyone else completing his final project. After all, he'd wanted me to burn his magic notebooks if I wasn't going to use them.

Of course, that last letter he'd left hadn't discussed his treasure hunting notes at all...

Wait. He'd left me another letter. The one to be opened if he was still alive.

He wasn't alive. Or at least, I didn't have any reason to think he would be. But what if that letter held a clue? Some information that could help me with all this?

Well, first things were first. I had to eat.

I scrambled up some eggs with cheese, sourdough toast and a few slices of bacon. Sat at my table with a glass of water, and ate while looking up Greek measures online.

Practically did a spit-take when I got my answer.

One talent weighed almost *sixty pounds*.

Fifty talents meant ... almost *three thousand pounds* of orichalcum.

None of those formulae needed less than six ounces or more than twelve to make their ambrosia.

Even allowing for some loss in initial experimentation, that meant that as many as *four thousand people* could be made *immortal*.

The implications were staggering. World-changing.

How could anyone possibly choose who was "worthy" of immortality and who wasn't? This was a matter beyond mere wealth or power, but it would be degraded to that level by any who found out about it.

Governments would try to seize it. Assassins and strike teams would try to claim it. Wars would be fought over it.

If anyone found out.

But how would one keep this quiet?

How did Uncle Charles keep any of his treasure hunting quiet? Patience, restraint and magic. He had left me treasures in that garage that people would kill for. So maybe his plan was to find the orichalcum and *not tell anyone*. Use bits of it to experiment with the formulae. Find out if any of them worked.

If they did, he'd be immortal. And then he'd have all eternity to pick and choose who else to grant immortality to.

Done slowly, over a long period of time, and choosing only the right people. Maybe that way, the world at large would never find out.

Obviously the right people had to be able to keep a secret. But what other qualities would he have looked for?

This was all speculation into darkness. It got me nowhere, and what I needed was direction. Some kind of clue I hadn't found yet. And the only place I could think to look was the other letter he'd left me.

18

Dear Charlie,

If you're reading this, then you felt something watching you, which means I'm still alive. It also means I'm in trouble, since I've been missing long enough for them to declare me dead.

Shocking news, huh? Trust me, wherever I am, I'm pretty shocked about it too. I'm a careful guy, by inclination, no matter what your dad says about me.

Safe to say I'm in a tight spot, and I need your help, old buddy.

Problem is, the kind of help I'm likely to need won't involve any of your current instincts. So don't call your dad. Don't go to the government. And don't go to Mr. McDonnell.

Right now you might be wondering why you shouldn't go to your dad. After all, he is my brother, and he'd want to help. But really, how can you convince him? You only know I'm alive because you feel a presence there in the room with you. And even if you bring your dad down there – a terrible idea, by the way – he won't feel it.

Your dad, he's not like us. He's more like your grandfather. He closes his eyes to anything that doesn't fit into the world as he sees it currently.

I'm not talking about politics, Charlie. I'm talking about the rules underwriting our reality. I'm talking about truths that fall between the cracks of the world as we're taught to see it.

I've spent my life probing those cracks for hidden truths. And while I've found some dead ends, I've learned some amazing things, Charlie. Things I can't wait to share with you.

Things your dad — or any of your other relatives, for that matter — would never believe.

Foremost among them? Magic.

It's real, Charlie. Not stage magic, but not Dungeons and Dragons *or* Harry Potter *magic either. The real thing. For example, I can conjure spirits and compel them to do things.*

You're probably scoffing at that idea. I wouldn't blame you, to be honest. I did too. At first.

Here's the thing, though, Charlie. You have an advantage that I didn't have. You already know it's true. Because that sense of being watched? Well, something is watching you. From that circle in the corner of the room, past the bookshelves.

It's my familiar, Nardis.

Try this, Charlie. Turn to that corner and say, "Nardis, in the name of my Uncle, Charles Warren, show yourself."

Even though I still felt no presence there, I turned to the corner and tried the words anyway.

Obviously they didn't work. I turned back to the letter.

Feeling all right, Charlie? Must've been quite a shock to suddenly see Nardis for the first time. A vaguely humanoid swirl of gray smoke with glowing purple eyes.

Still. Not bad, eh? Kind of nice to have proof so readily available.

Nardis helps me with my magic. Now, unfortunately, that's the only trick you can ask for that he'll grant. Because he's not your familiar. He's bound to me. And if he's there, I'm in tight enough straits that I can't call on him for help.

Which is why I need you to help me another way.

You're going to need to spend some money. Don't worry about that. Seriously. Blow as much as you need to. I can get more for both of us.

Now, you'll probably need to get into a fight with your dad. I know you won't want to do that, but it'll help make sure the family gives you space, while you do what needs doing.

Personally, I suggest telling them you aren't going into the family business. That should lead to a knock-down drag-out.

Next, I want you to go upstairs to my regular office. Knowing me, I've left it full of an intimidating array of maps, and notes you can't read. Don't worry about that right now. You'll have time to learn my cipher later.

The bottom right drawer of my desk in that office has a false back. That's where I keep my address book.

I know what you're thinking. That's a strange place for an address book. Well, Charlie, let's just say that the people in that book have reason to keep a low profile. So don't program any names or numbers from that book into your phone.

And right now, you only need one entry. Marjorie Kovacs. Commit her number to memory, then put the address book back.

When you call her, don't do it from your cell phone. I suggest picking up a cheap, prepaid mobile phone with international minutes, because you'll be calling someplace in Europe. If you have trouble finding that kind of phone, check the airport, near the international terminal. Should be easy enough there.

Once you have the phone, call her from a public place, like a café or mall or the airport, if you're already there. The point is, from someplace heavily trafficked and not close to your home.

Yes, I'm serious. Please do as I ask. I know it sounds strange. But I swear I have reasons, and I swear I'll explain them all when I see you.

When you speak to Marjorie, tell her your name, and that I'm in trouble and need help.

Now, she's going to ask you to come to Europe, Charlie. She won't discuss any details on the phone, so don't try to push for that. But trust me. She'll know what to do.

So grab some clothes, whatever you need, and get your butt on the first flight to wherever she says to meet her.

Don't charter a flight. Might draw attention. But fly first class. It's worth it.

Oh. Yes. Once you get off the phone with her, delete the number, break the sim card and throw away the phone. You won't need it again.

And do these things yourself, Charlie. Don't enlist McDonnell. For that matter, don't tell him I'm alive. Don't tell him anything you don't absolutely need to.

I know, I know. He's my lawyer. I trust him to ensure you get your inheritance, but not to get me out of a jam?

Well, my jam isn't a legal matter, or I'd've solved it myself. No, if you're reading this, I'm in a very tight spot. And until I know how I got here, best not to trust anyone you don't have to.

At least, anyone except Marjorie. Her you can trust implicitly.

That's all I can tell you right now, Charlie. At least, that will make any sense to you. There's more. There's so much more. But that's all going to have to wait until I see you.

I hope it's soon.

Love,

Uncle Charles

I almost started making plans for a trip to Europe. Had to stop and remind myself that Nardis wasn't in that corner, so Uncle Charles wasn't in some tight spot, waiting for me to save him.

But now I knew that M. Kovacs was Marjorie Kovacs, and that my instincts had been right. She was the person I needed to contact. And now I knew how.

19

———————

I SLEPT WELL THAT NIGHT, BUT I WOKE UP NERVOUS. I WAS TOLD TO contact this Marjorie Kovacs if Uncle Charles was alive. And she didn't sound like someone who liked to talk on the phone. What could I say to her that would make her take me seriously? How could I convey my problem in as few words as possible?

My morning meditation cleared that jumbled chaos from my head. My run helped too. Both because it had become a kind of meditation of its own, and because the streets were so icy I couldn't afford to pay attention to anything but the next step.

By the time I'd returned, showered, and eaten breakfast I felt good again. Maybe I didn't know what to say, but maybe I wouldn't need to. Maybe I'd get as far as, "I'm not sure what to do about my uncle's last treasure hunting project," and she'd give me some quick and easy answer.

Then again, maybe she'd just hang up on me and that would be that. But if she did, that would be kind of an answer too. If someone Uncle Charles said I could trust implicitly really didn't care about his treasure hunting, I'd be free to make my own decision about it.

And if that happened, I knew what I'd do.

I'd burn those notes and maps.

All right. Maybe I wouldn't actually *burn* them. Maybe I'd store them down in the basement. Or maybe in the garage, once I learned how to cast the right kind of protection spell on them.

But one thing I wasn't willing to do: sell a key link to potential *immortality* to the highest bidder. No. I'd call Mr. McDonnell and tell him I decided to do with them what Uncle Charles said I should do with his magic notebooks, if I didn't intend to use them. Burn them.

No. Check that. I'd tell him I already did it. Fait accompli. No chance to talk me out of it or undo it. The world would just have to live with the discoveries my uncle had made *during* his lifetime.

Honestly, it was tempting just to go that direction anyway. But Mr. McDonnell was a wild card. I didn't know what he knew and what he didn't. And if he thought I'd just broken his only link to immortality, well, I didn't know how he'd react.

I definitely wanted to consult at least one true friend of my uncle's before making a final decision. So I had to give this Marjorie Kovacs a call. Had to try her first. Even if all she did was hang up on me.

Speaking of friends, I kept my lunch date with Becky before calling Marjorie Kovacs. Both of us bundled up and eating our spicy lamb wraps on a cold, metal bench near the food cart pod, while the gray skies threatened to rain or snow, but never got around to it.

Becky wanted to gush about spending the coming weekend up at Timberline with a group of friends. Somebody's parents had a cabin, so it would be days filled with skiing and snowboarding and nights filled with hot chocolate and other kinds of fun.

Honestly, she was so excited about the trip that it wasn't much of a conversation. More like my listening while her enthusiasm bubbled over for an hour or so. I didn't mind. It was good to see her so happy. And I was pretty sure she was interested in one of the boys on the trip – Travis – though she talked around the idea. As though she either wasn't ready to admit her interest out loud, or was worried that I'd take it wrong.

Naturally, as we parted, I teased her about it. "Remember. Some guys aren't good at catching hints. So don't be afraid to hit Travis with a snowball, if you need to."

She flushed so bright a red she could've led Santa's sleigh through the worst snowstorm on record.

Once we parted ways, I got serious. Checked a couple of nearby convenience stores, but couldn't find a prepaid mobile phone with international minutes. Oh, I could get one with domestic minutes, then get my international minutes from a prepaid *phone card*. That would've been an easy option. But I was trying to stick to the letter of Uncle Charles' instructions.

So I hopped the MAX out to the airport.

Portland Airport is a big, comfortable place full of stores and restaurants that, by law, can't charge more for what they sell than they do in town. I've always thought it was a nice place to kill time while waiting for a flight out or an arrival in. More ... welcoming than other airports I'd seen. Not that I'd seen all that many.

That day, though, holiday travel was in full swing, and I had to deal with large crowds of people who'd clearly spent too long in airports and on planes. They had that combination of exhaustion and impatience that can be brutal if you cross it.

Maneuvering around them, physically, would be pretty easy for me now. Most travelers tended to herd as they made their way through the wide halls, although a few tried to skirt around the crowds. Then there were the workers. Police, administration (I think) and other airport employees, moving at their own unhurried pace as they went about their days.

Taking a moment to observe before plunging in, I could feel the movement of the different groups. Like currents. Nothing would be easier than sliding into the gaps and making my own way.

But these days, I was becoming aware on more levels than just the physical. And in focusing on the crowds as I had, I began to feel their emotions, too. Their stress and urgency and frustration and impatience and hunger and exhaustion. Especially from the herds and the skirters.

Their individual emotional states had bled into each other. Thickened the very air into a gestalt of anxieties that swept over me. A tide, trying to drag my emotions with it.

I slipped defensively into a meditative state. The tide swept over me. I remained still. Empty. Gave it nothing to catch on to. No more engagement than I gave any of my own thoughts and feelings that would bubble up during meditation.

This, though, was a new experience. I'd never before felt a crowd this way. I'd never before been assailed by the aggregate emotions of others. But I couldn't take time to think about it. Couldn't give that fact any attention, or my meditative state would collapse and the waves of that tide would break upon me and carry me away.

For now, there was only stillness inside me. I could feel the heat of the herd's passage. Smell their odors of sweat and travel and harsh perfumes overlaying the chemicals of the airport rug cleaners and the coffee and pastries of a nearby café.

Feeling ready, I let my feet carry me, body and mind, past the morass without engaging with it.

Traffic relaxed closer to the international terminal, then tightened again as I neared security.

I didn't need to pass through, though. Just eased my way to the side of the wide hall and began hunting for places that sold mobile phones with international minutes.

Found them in a vending machine, of all things.

The right kind of phone acquired, I found the nearest food court. Plastic tables, metal chairs, and lots of people eating a wide variety of foods. I took an empty table near the smell of greasy pizza and burnt coffee.

I glanced about, trying to look as though considering my dining options. Actually I was making sure no one was too close, nor paying me undue attention.

Yeah, I felt kind of paranoid doing it, but honestly, this felt like spy stuff.

I dialed the number.

The ringtone sounded different. Deeper and longer than I was used to, from American numbers. And with a slight echo.

It rang nine times before I heard the click of connection.

"Guten abend." A woman's voice, slightly husky.

"My name is Charlie Warren, nephew of—"

"I know who you are." I couldn't place her accent, but she didn't sound German. "It is crucial that we talk. Come to Berlin."

And she hung up.

Fourteen freaking words, and she hung up.

I seriously considered calling her back, but I had the feeling she wouldn't pick up. Shaking my head, I erased my call log and deleted the number.

Well, Uncle Charles had warned me. She wouldn't discuss anything on the phone. So I either had to go to Berlin, or...

Wait. She said it was *crucial* that we talk. And she didn't sound like a woman to mince words. Could she have been waiting for my call?

Well, looked like I was going to Berlin.

20

IT WAS FUNNY. I WAS AT THE FREAKING INTERNATIONAL TERMINAL, BUT my first instinct was to go home and comparison shop for plane tickets on my laptop.

But I didn't have to comparison shop anymore. Not for price, anyway.

So I found out who could get me a first class ticket on the next flight to Berlin, and bought it without worrying about the price.

All right. I *told myself* I wasn't worrying about the price. But the truth was, I'd been living my life pretty much unchanged, except that I lived in my own house now, instead of my parents' house. I'd barely touched my inheritance.

So I wasn't used to dropping that amount of money all at once. My heart was pounding and I felt sweat bead on my forehead as I handed over my credit card. And I think, deep down, part of me was worried it would get declined.

Old habits of thought. Something I'd need to work on.

Once I had the ticket squared away, I popped the sim card out of that new phone. Tossed the phone into the nearest garbage. Snapped the sim card, and tossed part of it into a different garbage can, and the other part into the second garbage can I saw after getting off the MAX station near my house.

Because, yes, I went home first. Packed a roller bag with clothes and my backpack with a few books and blank notebooks. Sent text messages to Becky and Jonathan that I'd be going out of town to see friends for a few days, then left my own phone plugged in and charging on my nightstand.

Last but not least, I gathered up the notes and maps that Uncle Charles had left out in the map room, and brought them down into the basement. I didn't put them with the orichalcum box, though. I hid them behind books in the library. Just in case.

Then I had a few hours to kill. The flight wasn't leaving until ten o'clock that night. I did some reading, but kept getting distracted. I was worried about this trip. My guts kept twisting and knotting, my knees kept bouncing.

I felt like I was taking some kind of dangerous step. Calling someone who didn't want to talk on the phone, so I had to fly *halfway around the world*. And I could, but that wasn't the point.

What kind of person keeps so low a profile that it's not safe to have their name and number in my phone? That to call her, I had to go to some pretty extreme lengths. And now I was flying to Berlin to see her. No coordination about when I would be arriving. Whether someone would meet me, or what.

I mean, I'd never been to Berlin. Hell, I'd barely been out of the country, apart from a few trips up to British Columbia. But I figured Berlin had to be a pretty bit city. Like New York big, or at least Chicago. Was I supposed to just land there, buy another disposable phone and call her again?

Spy stuff. No. Worse than spy stuff. Even James Bond always had a contact and maybe a password when he was sent to foreign shores.

Point is, if this Marjorie Kovacs is so worried about being observed by someone, what were the odds that just in calling her I'd put myself on their radar? Was I being watched even now? If so, by whom?

The government? Which one?

That way lay madness. I knew that. But it kept coming to mind, because really, how different was Uncle Charles from this Marjorie Kovacs? No computer in his house? I mean, I'd always had a phone number for him, but he was my uncle...

This line of thought was getting me nowhere. I could clear it with meditation, but maybe I shouldn't. Maybe there was a point to it.

After all, if I felt as though I were doing something dangerous, maybe what I needed to do was take precautions.

I did my evening rituals a little early that night. And I followed them by creating a one-use talisman, to protect me while traveling. I put the spell into a Saint Christopher medal that Grandma Teresa, Mom's mom, gave me.

I always kept it, because it was a present and I keep presents, but I'd never done anything more than put it on my keyring – I think she'd wanted me to wear it as a necklace – because Dad would've thrown a fit. He wasn't much of a Lutheran, but he would've raged at finding his own son doing something so "pagan" as "putting a human before God."

Yeah, those were actual quotes, from one of his old arguments with Grandpa Ivan.

In this case, it felt appropriate. Saint Christopher was supposed to protect travelers, so why not use his medal for my one-use protection talisman?

From there, I went through the house, making sure it was locked up. I double-checked the garage as well, then off to the MAX station and the airport. Better too early than too late, after all.

I quickly learned that Uncle Charles had the right of it. First class was definitely the way to go. Faster through security and customs. A neat little lounge, where I could wait for my flight away from any more exposures to emotionally powerful herds. Hadn't even gotten on a plane yet, and I knew I'd be flying first class from there on out.

It was a long flight. Changed planes in Seattle and Frankfurt. Some sixteen hours in all. Add to that the time change, and I lost just over a whole day to that trip.

But I have to admit, the seats were large and comfortable. I was even able to catch some sleep, which I'd never done before on a plane. And when I was awake, the flight attendants friendly and helpful. Heck, even the food was good. I had steak and eggs in there somewhere.

Eventually, though, I did arrive in Berlin.

Airport there made Portland's feel like a postage stamp. Everything was huge. The ceiling heights, the halls. Lots of mirrors and glass and echoing tile. And the travelers spoke a host of languages that made me feel like a dirty, ugly American who couldn't even recognize more than a half-dozen, if that. To say nothing of speaking most of them.

The fashions were different. The cuts of clothing. The hairstyles. I didn't just feel as though I'd crossed the globe. I felt as though I'd entered another world entirely, and I hadn't gone ten steps from my gate yet.

Fortunately, two things worked in my favor. First, most of the signs were in both German and English, and second, the symbol for "baggage claim" was pretty universal. I hadn't checked any bags, but I figured that baggage claim would be near the most convenient exit.

So I settled myself and took my time as I made my way toward baggage claim. I wanted to acclimate to the other strangeness I was dealing with.

Since beginning my study of magic, I hadn't left Portland. So as my ... less physical senses became more aware, I'd been unconsciously getting used to the *feel* of Portland. At that point, I didn't know how to describe that, even to myself, except that it felt like home. And even the Portland airport felt pretty much like Portland's open doorway.

But now I was in Berlin. Or at least at Berlin Brandenburg airport, and its feel was...

Exposed. Strange. Like going to sleep in your own bed, and waking up to realize you're *not* in your own bed. The mattress, the sheets, the blankets, the room around you. All *similar* in the way that they're still a mattress with sheets and blankets, in a room. But other than that, entirely different.

And this, this was *not* Portland on a very basic level. The sense of community was different. The sense of order and propriety. And beyond those things, the sort of genius locus they formed.

I was as constantly aware of the, well, *psychic* difference – for lack of a better word – the way I would be aware of stepping out of a cool, dry house into a hot, muggy afternoon. I would adjust, but it would take time.

I was still adjusting when I came past the security checkpoint and a man stepped in front of me. Not close enough to intrude on my space, but close enough to get my attention.

"*Herr* Warren, I believe?"

The man's voice was soft and his accent German, but his words as crisp as his black uniform. He was an older man. Silver-haired, but powerfully built, with reddish skin and pale blue eyes.

For a moment I wondered if he were some kind of policeman. But then I realized his hat was a chauffeur's hat.

"I'm Charlie Warren," I said softly, freely wearing my suspicion on my face and in my voice.

"Excellent." He clacked his heels together and gave me a small, sharp bow. "I am Ritter. *Frau* Kovacs sent me."

I sighed hard enough that I almost collapsed forward.

He smiled. "Nothing better than a friendly face when all is confusion, *Ja*? Might I take your bags?"

I only had the two, the roller and my backpack. "They aren't worth troubling you."

"No trouble at all. Please."

"Well, the roller, I guess," I said, and he took the handle without another word and led the way. He went right past baggage claim, even though he hadn't asked if I had any more luggage.

He didn't lead me toward the parking lots, either. His car was waiting at the curb, undisturbed among the tumult of people and traffic involved in leaving the airport.

The car was a BMW limousine. Seats I could have slept in, and dreamed of their rich leather scent.

"You should of course help yourself to anything you please, *Herr*

Warren," Ritter said, indicating the small fridge before closing the door.

The fridge held a selection of cheeses and sliced fruits, along with bottles of water – both still and sparkling – and beer.

I contended myself with some muenster and cheddar, with slices of apple and pear and a bottle of still water, while Ritter eased us away from the curb.

The traffic was thick, but seemed to melt around the car whenever Ritter needed to change lanes or turn. For that matter, the traffic signals seemed to hold their lights for him.

I realized then that it wasn't my imagination. I *was* feeling the presence of magic. The car was enchanted.

Well, then I'd definitely come to the right place.

21

———————

Under other circumstances, I might've rubbernecked at the windows, trying to see everything there was to see of Berlin during that drive. But now that I was getting close to finally meeting this Marjorie Kovacs, those espionage feelings were percolating again. Tightening lots of little muscles through my body. Making me wonder if eating something had been a mistake.

Ritter *said* he was from Marjorie—

No. He said he was from *Frau* Kovacs. Never said *Frau Marjorie* Kovacs. I'd just assumed. Of course, if she really kept her identity close to the chest, then that made a certain amount of sense.

But if she *needed* to keep her identity so quiet, then likely people were watching her. People who might want to pick up the strange American for questioning...

"Ritter?" I asked.

"*Ja?*" he answered, without looking back.

"How did you know when I would be arriving?"

"I myself did not know. *Frau* Kovacs told me to come collect you at twenty-three thirty, and so, I was there. I trust I did not keep you waiting?"

"No, not at all," I said. "But ... how did *she* know? She never asked for my flight information."

Ritter chuckled. "I believe you know the answer to that."

Magic. Duh.

"Yes," I said, "but what kind? Do you know?"

"She does not take me into her confidence about such things. Surely you did not attempt to *hide* your itinerary from her?"

"Well, no..."

"Good. She would not have appreciated that."

None of this was helping my nerves.

"Do you know why she doesn't like to talk on the phone?"

"It is unfortunate that the questions you choose to ask are ones I cannot answer for you."

I chuckled helplessly. "Sorry. Long flight."

"I have no doubt of it. But I am certain you will have all your answers soon."

I spent most of the rest of the drive in meditation. When I finally opened my eyes, we were no longer in Berlin. Or any city, for that matter. We were speeding along a freeway. I thought about asking where we were and where we were going, but I didn't see the point. I didn't know the layout of Germany.

If we were even staying in Germany. For all I knew, she'd had me fly to Berlin so she could have me driven somewhere else. Heck, Mr. McDonnell had sent her mail to somewhere in Denmark...

"Ritter, are we still in Germany?"

"*Ja. Frau* Kovacs' estate is not far now. Pity you arrived at night. You are missing the beautiful countryside."

True. But then, the heavy rain was likely a factor there too. It was pouring down pretty hard. Apart from the freeway, the main thing I could tell was that we were driving through a hilly area.

Finally he took an exit, and a short time later, a series of turns, and then we were on a narrow road, unlit but for the headlights. We were driving through woods now, among firs, pines, alders and yews that I could pick out close to the road.

We reached a clearing, passed through an iron gate in a tall stone wall, and came through the clearing into more hilly forest. Or maybe forested hills. Either way, we tracked their curves.

I spotted a house off to the left. We didn't stop.

Another, off to the right this time. We didn't stop.

We passed another couple of buildings that I was increasing less certain were houses.

Finally I saw the mansion. And it was a *mansion*. All lit up, both inside and out. The kind of place where the designers decided they couldn't cram the family into a mere ten thousand square feet spread across three floors, so they had to build wings.

Wings.

Whole Portland city blocks would've fit into this place. The sheer number of nails and screws that went into it must've been staggering. A small forest must've died for the lumber.

Gods, just getting the *windows* contract for that place could've turned a struggling company into a powerhouse in the market.

Somebody made their *career* on that behemoth. Maybe more than one person.

Between us and this spectacle of a house was a circle wide enough for even a long limo like this one to turn figure eights with room to spare. In the center of the circle, a moderate-sized park, complete with benches, fountains, and a flower garden.

Ritter pulled right up to the blue stone steps that led up to the tall, wide, arched double doors of the mansion.

I moved to exit the limo and my door was opened by a tall, uniformed man who looked handsome enough to be walking a runway somewhere, instead of holding an umbrella for me.

As I got out of the limo he took my backpack from me. "I will see to it that your bags are brought to your rooms, *Herr* Warren."

I was too surprised to object. Or maybe too tired. Or maybe still dealing with that fish-out-of-water sensation. Hell, probably all three and a few other things besides.

Wait. Did he say *rooms*? Plural?

Before I could ask, he escorted me to the open front door, where a butler bowed to me. More pristine posture, this time from a man who looked old enough to remember World War I, but his dark eyes still looked lively, and his voice sounded strong and unaccented when he spoke.

"On behalf of your hostess, it is my great pleasure to welcome you to Kovacs Abbey, *Herr* Warren."

"Thank you..." I said, letting the words hang, expecting him to introduce himself.

He didn't.

"*Frau* Kovacs awaits you with a light supper in the burgundy room, but you may refresh yourself first, if you like."

"No need," I said. "I'd very much like to meet *Frau* Kovacs."

"But of course. This way."

Well, no one could say that Kovacs stinted on her interior. The air was scented gently with ... something floral. Pleasant without being sweet. The tile looked Italian and expensive, and went well with the kind of fancy wallpaper that I knew cost even more than it looked.

And then there was the artwork.

Statues that looked as though they could've been done by Rodin. Paintings I was *sure* had been done by the likes of Goya, Da Vinci and other masters. And that wasn't all. The corners of the rooms – even the huge entry hall, with its immense real-crystal chandelier – looked *perfectly* squared. So good I half-wanted a level so I could check them.

The burgundy room was up a curving staircase made from a black heartwood. Clean lines and gentle curves. Just admirable work-manship, every detail.

The hall I was led down had a flooring that looked like Brazilian Tigerwood, overlain with a runner carpet with an elaborate design in reds and oranges. Recessed alcoves in the golden wallpaper high-lighted small, lit portraits of people I didn't recognize.

I was no expert in art, but even I could tell that they'd all been done by different artists, and over a fair stretch of time. At least a couple of hundred years.

The burgundy room wasn't named for the color. It had the same tigerwood flooring and gold wallpaper.

Wait. Not quite. The gold wallpaper in here had relief patterns of some kind.

Twin dark, antique bookcases on one wall featured books in a wide variety of sizes and designs, none of which looked as though they'd been published anytime in the last hundred years.

The wall art involved both landscape tapestries and paintings that looked like depictions of historical moments. A meeting between monarchs and their courts. A look at a battlefield after the battle, with one armored knight triumphant. That kind of thing.

In the center of the room, more dark, antique furniture. A smallish rectangular table, surrounded by four padded armchairs. The table was set for one, with a plate, silverware and a crystal goblet that all had to have been as old as the table they sat on. In the center of the table, a trio of covered silver platters.

The woman rising from her seat at the opposite end of the table from the place setting was, I presumed, Marjorie Kovacs.

I wasn't sure what I'd been expecting. Maybe some tall, striking femme fatale type. But that wasn't this woman.

She was short. Hardly an inch over five feet tall. Slight enough that I almost imagined I could pick her up with one hand. She wore a navy blue skirt suit that looked to have been threaded here and there with silver. Her black curls had been tamed into good behavior, falling somewhere close to her shoulders, framing delicate features.

But there was nothing delicate about those hazel eyes. They seemed to radiate power. In fact, after that first glance I found myself thinking of her as larger than she was. As though she actually took up a good deal more space than her body realized. And she practically vibrated with health and vigor.

I had no sense of age from her. She could have claimed to be either twenty or fifty and I wouldn't have been able to tell if she were lying.

Her smile was reassuring, though, and I recognized that accent I couldn't place when she spoke.

"Ah, Charlie Warren. You look just as I imagined you. Welcome. I, of course, am Marjorie Kovacs."

She extended her hand, and for the life of me, I wasn't sure if I should shake it or kiss it.

I shook it, and if that surprised her, I couldn't tell. But she had a cool, firm grip.

"Please," she said, gesturing to the place setting. "Sit. I shall serve you myself."

That sounded like an honor I shouldn't refuse, so I sat on the offered chair while she uncovered platters long enough to give me a slice of grilled salmon with some kind of sauce, asparagus with – most likely – hollandaise sauce, and buttered rye bread. She also poured white wine into my goblet, and gestured to a small series of silver bowls.

"Blackberry, raspberry, and blueberry jam, should you wish them."

"Thank you," I said as she took her seat while hunger seized me and I realized I hadn't eaten anything but a small snack since that steak and eggs. But my manners came to the fore and I looked at her own lack of plate or goblet.

"Forgive me for not joining you in your repast," she said with a smile. "But I prefer to take nothing between twenty and eight."

"Twenty..." I said, picking up my utensils. "Oh, twenty hundred hours."

"Just so," she said, and gave me an expectant look.

"If I could ask..."

"You have come a long way to do so."

"Why the secrecy around your name and phone number?"

"That is an interesting question," she said with an enigmatic smile. "But not the question you have come so far to ask."

"Yes, but—"

"Eat first. Then we will discuss the question you came to ask. After which we may discuss a great many things."

22

———————

AT FIRST, I THOUGHT IT MIGHT BE AWKWARD FOR US TO SIT IN SILENCE while I ate. But the silence of Marjorie Kovacs was surprisingly companionable. Not only didn't I feel uncomfortable – as though I should say something, just to break the silence – but I found myself relaxing while I enjoyed my meal.

And it was a surprisingly good meal. Especially considering I was sure they couldn't have known exactly when I was arriving. Which suggested that the chef had done an excellent job of keeping it warmed just right.

The salmon fillet was light and juicy, under a tangy citrus sauce that could have been designed around the chablis. The hollandaise was best I'd ever had, and really made the asparagus a marvelous counterpoint. I almost felt guilty eating the rye bread, but it seemed like the perfect choice to keep the sauces from feeling too rich to my bland, American palate.

Once I was done, I opened my mouth to speak, but Marjorie Kovacs held up a hand. She said something in German, and the butler whisked in with a pair of maids and cleared the table.

They must've been waiting just outside the door.

The butler returned, stepped just inside the door, and closed it.

He stood facing the room, with his hands behind his back. I hoped that was to ensure our privacy and not for ominous reasons.

"Now," Marjorie Kovacs said, "I believe there is a question you would like to ask me."

"Why did you say it was crucial that we talk?"

"Because it is, for reasons I shall make clear later. First, your question, if you would."

"Perhaps he would prefer a night's rest first?" the butler said. "His day has been quite long."

"Under other circumstances I would agree," she replied. "But in this instance, I think now is better."

"I slept on the plane anyway," I said, then drew a deep breath. I looked at her a trifle suspiciously. She didn't look suspicious. She regarded me with seemingly infinite patience. But I couldn't help it. This all seemed so ... planned. Like I was playing a role in someone else's game...

Still. Uncle Charles said I could trust this woman implicitly.

One more deep breath, and I began.

"All right. You're aware, I believe, that my uncle disappeared from the Caribbean Sea, somewhere near Puerto Rico. Correct?"

"So I was informed by your uncle's attorney, one Daniel McDonnell, esquire."

"And do you know why I believe he is not just missing, but dead?"

"Mr. McDonnell informed me that you had confirmation of your uncle's death, not the nature of that confirmation. Is it germane to your question?"

I thought about that for a moment. "No. I suppose not."

Her eyebrows moved in a gesture I could only take as encouragement to continue.

"Do you know what my uncle was doing when he disappeared?"

"I know entirely what your uncle was doing when he disappeared."

That startled me into narrowing my eyes at her. "That sounds fairly ... complete. You're certain you know so much?"

"Your uncle consulted with me on a great many subjects. Including his last sea voyage."

"You might know more than I do, then."

"Most assuredly," she said. "Perhaps it would be faster if you told me what you do know about it."

"But if we both know, I can go straight to the point, which is—"

"Ah, but do we both know the same things? I was taken into your uncle's confidence on this matter. Can you say the same?"

"I have his maps and notes."

"And what have they told you?"

"I thought I was supposed to be the one asking the big question."

"You are," she said casually. "But context is important for any question. Lay the foundation for me, so that I might understand your view of the matter, and be better able to answer your question."

I reminded myself again that Uncle Charles had made clear I could trust her implicitly, even when his life was on the line.

Plus, it had been *her* surname on one of those manuscript files.

"All right," I said. "Cards on the table. My uncle was after a shipment of orichalcum that had sunk on its way to Athens. Fifty talents of it."

"Should I presume you refer to the alloy known to numismatists?"

"No," I said, looking her squarely in the eye. "I am referring to Atlantean orichalcum. The true metal. And I'm pretty sure you know why he wanted to find it."

"I would imagine such a find would be worth quite a bit of money," she said, her face and eyes both absent of any hints about whether she knew more than that.

But I already knew she did.

"It's worth more than money, and you know why."

"What makes you say so?"

"My uncle consulted an ancient manuscript belonging to someone named Kovacs. It was one of the manuscripts that presented him with formulae for purifying orichalcum into its original form."

"Which is?"

"Ambrosia."

She didn't even bat an eye.

"Worth more than money indeed, if true. So what is the question you have come here to ask me, Charlie Warren?"

"Mr. McDonnell wants me to let him sell my uncle's research into the location of that shipment. He claims not to know what my uncle was after, that it's just one more valuable treasure hunt to cash in on. But I'm not so sure. He sounds sometimes like he knows more than he's letting on."

"What is your question?"

"My uncle said that if I wasn't going to study his magic, I should burn his notebooks. But he didn't say anything at all about his treasure hunting notes." I shook my head and sighed. "I don't know that I have what it takes to go treasure hunting like my uncle did. I don't know that I *should*. I mean, if even one of those formulae works, that shipment represents enough ambrosia to make *thousands* of people *immortal*."

Just saying that aloud to another human being made me feel exhausted. I hung my head.

"I just don't know if I have what it takes to handle something like that. The responsibility. Plus the danger, if anyone found out."

"The danger to you?"

"The danger to the world! Could you imagine a dictator or would-be dictator getting their hands on *ambrosia*? The robber-baron CEOs? The personality cultists? This could lead to wars. New religions. Widespread oppression on a global scale. One mistake could unleash all kinds of hell on earth."

"So what will you do?" she asked.

"That's the question. I'm torn between burying that research in hopes that I feel up to going after that shipment someday. When I'm older and wiser and maybe up to the task."

"Torn between that and what?"

"And just *burning* those notes and maps, and hoping no one else ever finds that shipment."

"I don't hear a question."

"I think you must've known my uncle better than I did. What would he want me to do?"

She tilted her head and looked at me curiously. "If I were to tell you, you would do it?"

"No," I said. "I would take my uncle's view into account, but I would make my own decision in the end."

"Wonderful, Charlie!" A voice said from behind me. "You've done a perfect job of it. And given the best answer I could have hoped for!"

And I knew that voice.

It was my uncle's.

23

———

I JUMPED OUT OF THAT ANTIQUE CHAIR SO FAST IT TIPPED OVER AND fell backwards across the tigerwood floor. I whipped around. Every nerve screaming. Every muscle tight. Every sense on high alert.

But there he stood. Beaming at me like I'd hit a walk-off home run in Little League.

My Uncle Charles. Alive and well.

And it was definitely him. The eyes. The smile. The simple clothes. Levi 501s with a red plaid felt shirt and sneakers, as though he were just swinging by the house to say hi on his way to another great adventure.

I just stared, slack-jawed. Heart pounding. The world going red around the edges and tunneling down. Tilting off kilter...

"Breath, Charlie," Uncle Charles said, stepping closer. "Slow, deep belly breaths. Like I taught you."

Whether it was his advice or the habit built through training, I felt myself doing just that. Taking those slow, deep breaths, from the pit of my stomach to the upper tip of my lungs.

While I did this, Uncle Charles picked up my chair.

"Had you expected so vigorous a response, Charles?" Marjorie Kovacs said, sounding both blasé and still seated. "If so, you might've warned me. I'd rather not have to have that chair refinished."

"It's fine," Uncle Charles said, after a brief examination. Then to me, he added, "And so are you. Take your seat, Charlie."

"You're not dead," I said dully. "But ... your familiar..."

"Yes, Nardis is here with me. Please do sit. I'll explain everything."

"Some water for the young man," Marjorie Kovacs said to her butler, and he retrieved it so quickly I had only just sat down when he poured me a glass of water and left the carafe.

"Now, Charlie," my apparently-not-dead uncle said, "I'm sorry to have tricked you this way. I truly am."

"But there's no other door," I said, craning my neck and looking around. "Where—"

"I've in the room the whole time," Uncle Charles said. "There are ways to make people ignore your presence."

"I've got to tell Dad," I said. "And Grandpa and Grandma. And—"

"You'll do no such thing," he said firmly. "I don't like making them think I'm dead, but it's *necessary*. I wasn't even one hundred percent certain I could tell *you* the truth. Not until I heard what you had to say."

"But why? Why fake your death?"

"Look at me, Charlie. Really look at me."

I did, and saw what he meant. Healthy. Vibrant. Like Marjorie Kovacs. And more than that. He looked years younger. Decades, maybe. He'd've been believable as my older brother.

"Suppose I show up for new year's," he said. "What will everyone say about that fact that I look more like your cousin now, than your uncle?"

"They'll say you've had work done."

"And what will they say when ten years pass and I look no older?"

"You found it," I breathed. "And it's real? Ambrosia?"

"Yes. Which is why I had to disappear. The world has to believe that Charles Warren is dead."

"You could've shared it with your family."

"And tell me truly. Could *any* of them have kept the secret?"

I wanted to challenge that, but knew I couldn't. Mom. Dad. Jonathan. Grandma and Grandpa on both sides. None of them could've kept something like this quiet for a week, let alone a lifetime. And while the world at large might not believe them, all it would take would be one wrong person investigating...

"That's right," Uncle Charles. "I couldn't risk word getting out, and you've already listed some of the reasons why. Thus, a faked death."

"Done in such a way as to discourage investigation," Marjorie Kovacs added.

I frowned. "So ... my 'inheritance.' It was all a test, wasn't it?"

"Yes and no," Uncle Charles said. "If you'd never taken it any further, I still wanted you to live out your days in comfortable luxury. I don't mind admitting you've always been my favorite nephew."

"But I didn't stop there."

"No, you didn't. You began practicing magic, following the regimen I set for you. And you've done an excellent job of that. That protection spell in your pocket is a good one."

"Yes," Marjorie Kovacs said. "I meant to compliment you on it earlier. Quite well done, for someone of less than a year's experience."

"Thank you," I said, trying to keep up with it all.

"And you didn't just study my magic. You took up the test. You looked over the clues I left you. The maps and notes. You didn't just trash them or sell them. You showed the kind of curiosity I'd always *believed* you had, but needed proof. You dug through my orichalcum research."

He grinned at me. "You even did your best to translate those manuscript pages."

"How did you know that?"

"I've had you under observation, of course. Your senses are coming along well, but you're not advanced enough to always detect a spirit congruent with other magics around you, let alone notice when someone's scrying on you."

That gave me a shiver. The thought that Uncle Charles had been spying on me. And I'd made it easier on him, because ... "I did all that orichalcum work down in the magic workshop."

Uncle Charles wiggled his eyebrows at me, so familiar a gesture that I laughed without thinking. He wasn't spying on me. He was monitoring me while I took a test.

"You worked out for yourself what I'd been up to," Uncle Charles said. "And when you understood, you didn't get greedy or short-sighted. I hadn't *thought* you would, but one must be sure about these things. Instead, you labored over the ramifications and potential ramifications. And in the end, you did what I hoped you'd do. Consulted Marjorie here."

"What if I hadn't? What if I'd tried to go looking myself?"

"I would've met you at sea, of course," Uncle Charles said, laughing. "Couldn't have you wasting your time looking for what I'd already found."

"So you have all that orichalcum?"

"Not fifty talents worth, I'm afraid. A fair amount of it was scattered in the ocean's depths. I recovered maybe a third."

"That's still enough to make..." I tried running the numbers in my head.

"Allowing a certain portion for other uses," Marjorie Kovacs said, "enough to make nine hundred twelve people immortal."

I looked at her sharply. "So the working formula is yours?"

"Yes," she said, giving me the most direct answer I'd had from her yet. "I worked out the process myself when I came into possession of a small portion of true orichalcum a good many years ago. Would you care to guess where and when?"

She made a point of looking around the room.

"This is the burgundy room," I said. "Named not for the color but ... for the *country*?"

"Very good."

"So ... what ... twelfth century?"

"Eleventh. But closer, I confess, than I expected."

"Wait," I said, hands coming up to my forehead. This was all just too much. That meant this woman was close to a *thousand* years old. Ambrosia wasn't just real, it was *real*. True immortality.

Heck, Marjorie Kovacs — if that *was* her real name — barely looked thirty. If that. And she practically vibrated with good health. And she'd probably look exactly the same in another *thousand* years. And now, so would Uncle Charles. Who wasn't dead at all. Who might now *never* die...

"Breathe, Charlie," Uncle Charles said gently. "Breathe. Take your time."

"Perhaps actually drinking some of that water would help," Marjorie Kovacs said, so I did. Calmness washed through me, relaxing both muscles and mind.

I looked at the water glass.

"Oh, he *is* good," Marjorie Kovacs said with a smile. "Tell me. Did you sense it? Or deduce it?"

"Deduce. I think."

"That's fine at your stage," she said. "Possibly preferable. Do you know what I did?"

"You made the water more ... soothing."

"Exactly what I did before your arrival. 'Soothing' is just the right word, for English. Water is a perfect vessel for such, because it is the element of water that is best used to soothe a troubled mind."

"Sleep will be better still," Uncle Charles said.

"But wait," I said. "What about Mr. McDonnell?"

"What about him?" Uncle Charles asked, then chuckled. "Oh. The notes and maps?"

I nodded. "I think he knows what you were really after. Or at least suspects."

"Well, that hardly matters now," he said, shrugging one shoulder. "Sell them to him. Or through him. Whatever. Assuage his concerns and let some fool pay you for the privilege of hunting for my leavings. They won't find much, if anything at all. Just translate the notes first, so they don't learn my cipher."

"Feels dishonest."

"Not at all," Uncle Charles said. "The world believes me dead anyway, and a great many treasure hunts lead to nothing."

"But your reputation."

"The sooner my reputation dies, the better," Uncle Charles said firmly. "Let them stop talking about me."

"There is another reason," Marjorie Kovacs said. "If you do not sell the research, anyone who knows of the hunt and even *suspects* the true nature of orichalcum might wonder if your uncle found that shipment after all, and simply disappeared. Might go looking for him."

"Good point," Uncle Charles said.

"I guess so," I said, shaking my head. "I'll contact Mr. McDonnell when I get home."

"Which means you should go home soon," Marjorie Kovacs said. And when Uncle Charles opened his mouth to object, she continued, "I have no wish to make of myself a poor hostess by expelling a guest after only one night's stay. But this is a matter best dealt with expediently, and in person."

"She's right," I said.

"Besides, Charles," Marjorie Kovacs said with a smile. "If you wish, you could have all the time in the world to spend with your nephew."

My heart practically lurched to a stop. "I..."

"No need to finish that sentence, Charlie," Uncle Charles said gently. "You've passed my test, and I'm more than willing to give you a taste of ambrosia. But not for another few years. If my guess is right, the ambrosia restored me to about twenty-eight, which means that's the age it considers prime. Hate to see you get shorted by tasting it too soon."

"It could be that the ambrosia will allow him to age to that point and no further," Marjorie Kovacs said, her voice almost clinical.

"I'll wait," I said, before Uncle Charles could answer. "I'm not ready."

Uncle Charles nodded and gave me a proud smile. "Another worthy answer."

24

———

It's funny. I know that the suite of rooms I had that night at Marjorie Kovac's estate represented the kind of opulent luxury that a guy like me had only ever seen in movies. I remember that I had something like four or five rooms all to myself – including a private bathroom bigger than my living room back home – each of them complete with fancy antique furnishings and all that went with them.

But the truth is, I barely noticed any of the details. Even after a second glass of the house special soothing water, my head was still spinning.

Uncle Charles was *alive*.

He'd found that orichalcum. Some of it, anyway.

He'd successfully produced *ambrosia* from it.

And now ... now he was *immortal*.

My dead uncle was alive. And now he would live forever.

And so, apparently, would his girlfriend. Or colleague, maybe. I didn't know *what* the relationship was between my uncle and Marjorie Kovacs.

Marjorie Kovacs, who'd been born in the *eleventh fucking century*.

I think I lost nearly fifteen minutes to a spasm of laughter, thinking that if they were lovers, she was robbing the cradle on a truly epic scale. I know that when I came back to my senses, I was on the marble floor of the bathroom.

My magic was good enough to get me a free, home-baked chocolate muffin. Maybe to keep me safe while traveling.

My *uncle's* was good enough to make him *immortal*.

Well, all right. Technically that was alchemy, not magic, per se. But the distinction was splitting hairs pretty fine.

And now ... now I could become immortal too. I could taste real ambrosia. The food of the gods.

Immortality, I went back and forth on. Maybe Uncle Charles could just walk away from our family, but he'd been the black sheep for a long time. Me, though, I wasn't sure I could do it.

Yeah, I didn't see eye-to-eye with Jonathan on much of anything. I fought with Dad more than talked with him. And Mom might've accepted me but she never understood me. But they were still my family. And I still loved them.

I wasn't sure I could just ... fake my death and go on without them. Not today. But not in a decade, either. Maybe never.

I mean, it sounds kind of cool to think of staying young and healthy forever. But what kind of a life is it really? Everyone around you still dies. Family. Friends. Lovers. Children, if you have any. Unless you make them immortal. But even then, what guarantee is that of living happily ever after?

Couples split up all the time. Families argue and stop talking. Becoming immortal doesn't change any of that. Oh, sure, you've got a lot longer to get over things and come back together. That's true enough. But as years begin to pass like seconds and centuries like hours, holding a grudge might last a millennium. Or longer.

And there's still just the one earth. At the rate we're going, with climate change and pollution, how habitable will this place be in five hundred years? A thousand years? Ten thousand?

Seems like choosing immortality is going all-in on exploring space. Otherwise, what happens when earth's air isn't breathable and there's nothing to eat?

No. I wasn't sure at all that I wanted to be immortal.

But damn if I wasn't curious about ambrosia.

What did it look like? Smell like? Taste like? Was it chewy? Crisp? Sticky? Did it melt on the tongue or slide smoothly down the throat? What did it feel like in the stomach? Was any part of it considered waste by the body?

That was where the real problem lay for me, and I knew it. Chances were, Uncle Charles had some quantity of ambrosia with him. If I asked, he would show it to me. Or at least describe it for me.

And if that happened, I'd be sunk. Because I'd have to know. I'd *have* to. How could I not?

At that point in my deliberations, I stopped and did my nightly rituals.

One of my rooms was set up for that. Simple black floor and white walls. Simple oak cabinets, full of any equipment I might not have brought with me. But I didn't need any, not at my stage. Not for what I was doing.

No. My nightly rituals included incantations, gestures, and poses, but that was about it.

So I performed what I thought of as the personal cleansing ritual first. Uncle Charles' notebooks had called it a 'banishing ritual,' but so far as I could tell, the only things it banished were astral effluvia. Made me feel more like I'd had the magical equivalent of a good shower.

One of the nice side-effects, though, was a balancing and centering element. Helped get me back on level ground, mentally, after the shocks of my evening.

Next came connecting myself to the essence of the Overworld and the Underworld, and channeling their energies into the power centers of my astral and etheric bodies. This part developed those bodies, as well as improving both my personal power and my ability to channel power.

I always loved that part, because the afterglow was kind of heady.

Next came my nightly meditation, seated cross-legged on the floor.

Once I finished, I was finally in a state to get some sleep. Theoretically. Honestly, though, it was still something like four or five in the afternoon, far as my body was concerned. Even though I felt exhausted mentally, and strung out from the travel, I couldn't just go to bed.

So I went back to that magic room and started running. I'd do ten laps one direction, then swap and do another ten the other direction, then swap again and so on. Strangely, my body thanked me for this. Or maybe that was just the runner's high that kicked in after a couple of hundred laps.

Either way, once I was done running I felt ready for a shower and at least a nap. Maybe a catnap. Maybe even just closing my eyes for a few minutes.

I was out as soon as my head hit the pillow.

25

I WOKE SOMEWHERE ABOUT EIGHT IN THE MORNING ACCORDING TO THE clock on my antique nightstand. I performed my morning rituals, then got dressed. I took a quarter from my wallet, and made of it a one-use talisman to support my staying centered. Just in case I got hit with any more surprises, or needed to make any snap decisions.

Putting that quarter in my pocket made me feel better right away. Though some of that was likely placebo effect. Still, it meant I could smile as I emerged from my bedroom to see about breakfast.

I'd just entered what was most likely the sitting room of my suite when a young maid curtsied to me.

"Good morning, *Herr* Warren. *Frau* Kovacs extends her regrets that she has been called away for work and will not see you before you leave. She wishes me to tell you that she is pleased to make your acquaintance, and that she hopes you will call on her in the future."

"Please thank her for me," I said.

"With pleasure," she said. "Your uncle breaks his fast on the grand balcony, and invites you to join him, should you feel so inclined."

"Where is that?"

"Allow me," she said with another curtsy, then led me out of my suite and down two long halls to a room whose south wall appeared to be entirely windows. Well, apart from the French doors, which she opened for me.

Grand balcony was right. Marjorie Kovacs could've hosted a two-hundred-person party out here, without it feeling cramped.

It swept the whole width of the main part of the house, from wing to wing, and extended maybe twenty-five or thirty feet over the lands below, which included a hedge maze, a series of gardens, between the house and the woods. Checkerboard tile flooring polished so it gleamed. The thick railing looked like marble, including the arches of its own supports, and the pillars holding up the balcony roof.

All the furniture looked antique, too. Wrought iron, mostly, either enameled or painted white. Though the padding on the seats and benches looked fairly modern.

Uncle Charles sat at a smaller table, near a breakfast buffet that was way too much for the two of us. A selection of fruits and melons, crepes and breads, omelets, sausages and bacon and more. Not to mention the drinks. Water and four kinds of juice: orange, apple, grape and ... grapefruit, I thought. Plus champagne, if anyone wanted mimosas.

A manservant stood behind the buffet. Perhaps ready to make those mimosas.

"Morning, Charlie," Uncle Charles said, smiling from his seat. "Just tell Karl there what you want and take a seat. He'll bring it to you."

"I think I can..." I started, but Karl gave me a gentle shake of his head.

Apparently serving myself would've been rude.

"All right," I said. "How about an omelet, bacon, a mixture of fruits and melons, and two crepes, if you would be so kind."

"But of course," Karl said. "And to drink?"

"Orange juice, please."

Karl didn't respond verbally, but began assembling my order. Uncle Charles nodded to the empty seat. When I sat, he said softly, "Marjorie's idea of being progressive is not requiring her staff to address us as *mein herr*. Best not to interfere with the way she has them run things."

"I'd imagine after a certain age, the decay of manners gets to you."

"Guess I'll find out," Uncle Charles said with a chuckle.

"Aren't you worried about that?" I asked. "I mean, the way the world is going—"

"I love adventure, Charlie. I live for it. Yes, I have set myself the greatest challenge imaginable. But that only excites me all the more."

I laughed. "You'll be one of the first people settling Mars, won't you?"

"First? Probably not. But I'll definitely go there. Humanity always finds a way, Charlie. Even when things look blackest. Remember that."

"I'll try," I said, as Karl set down my food and Uncle Charles gave his order. When he was done I continued, "I spent most of the night thinking about the downsides of immortality."

"I'd think less of you if you didn't," Uncle Charles said. "This is not a decision to take lightly."

"Well, I'm not in a hurry."

"No need to be," Uncle Charles said. "Marjorie was well into her fifties when she tasted ambrosia. The only downside to delay is the risk of your dying in some accident."

"What about illness or crippling injury?"

He gave me a frank look, while Karl set his breakfast before him and retreated to behind the buffet.

"Oh. Right," I said. "In the myths, ambrosia gets used to heal people. Doesn't it?"

He nodded, and we both tucked in. Again, the food was amazing. Marjorie Kovacs clearly didn't stint on her meals. The fruits and melons were perfectly ripe. The bacon just the kind of crisp I like, without being overdone. The omelet was dripping with three kinds of cheese, as well as shallots and spinach. The crepes were light, dusted gently with sugar and lemon.

Once we'd eaten our fill and the dishes were cleared away, Uncle

Charles handed me a small slip of paper. "My new phone number and a mailbox, in case you need them."

I tucked the paper into my pocket. "I take it this information goes into your address book, not my phone?"

"Very good," he said. "Each of the names in that book represents a person who has a reason to avoid scrutiny. But the only ones you *really* need are mine and Marjorie's."

"You don't need it back?"

"I've long since memorized those names and numbers."

I looked out over the grounds. Watched the wind play among the conifers in the distance.

I turned back to Uncle Charles. He regarded me with patient expectation.

I shook my head. "I don't even know where to start."

"Anywhere is fine."

"You're *alive*."

"I think we've covered that," he said with a smile.

"And immortal?"

"Watch." He pulled out a pocket knife and cut his arm. A shallow cut, but still. It didn't bleed. Just closed itself up. The blade, itself, was clean.

"You don't bleed?"

"I don't have blood anymore. If I were to cut deep enough, I might drip a bit of ichor."

"Ew," I said, without thinking.

He laughed. "I know the likes of Lovecraft and King have absconded with that word and made of it something gross. But originally it was what the Olympian gods bled."

"But you're not a god. Right?"

"Nope," he said, folding up his knife and putting it away. "Just an immortal."

"But if ambrosia is real, does that mean that the Olympian gods are real?"

"Not necessarily," he said casually. "Could just be humans who got their hands on purified orichalcum and became immortals."

"There are others out there. Aren't there?"

"A handful that I know of. Likely more that I don't."

The butler emerged from the French doors. "*Junger herr*, the car is ready to take you to your flight."

"Already?" Uncle Charles said bitterly.

"*Frau* Kovacs was quite clear that we were to see the young man safely onto the first flight back to Portland, Oregon. That requires that he leave now."

"But I haven't packed," I said, standing.

"That matter has been tended to," the butler said. "This way please."

He did at least give me time to hug my uncle before I left.

26

———————

Home again, home again, jiggety jig.

I mean, I'd known before I left that this was not going to a vacation. I wasn't going to spend two weeks or a month in Germany, seeing the sights. I was going there to accomplish a task, and then come home.

But wow. Weird to think that I'd flown all that way to spend maybe ten hours in Germany. Several of them asleep, and at least one of them at an airport.

Definitely worth it, though.

When I got home, before I even unpacked, I picked up my phone from the bedroom, grabbed a seat at the kitchen table, and called Mr. McDonnell.

"Charlie!" he said, sounding only a touch less avuncular than normal. "You're calling with good news, I hope?"

"Yes," I said. "Or at least, I hope so. I've been giving a lot of thought to what you've been telling me, and I think you're right. I think my uncle would've wanted me to sell his maps and notes for whatever I could get from them."

Thought? He'd told me so in as many words!

"Wonderful! Shall I send a messenger over to get them?"

"I could have the maps ready for you now. The notes will take me a day or two to type up."

"Don't do that," he said quickly. "His original handwritten notes will fetch a far higher price."

"They're written in a cipher. I'll need to translate them."

"You could provide a key."

"No," I said firmly. Perhaps the first time I'd taken a firm tone with Mr. McDonnell. "The cipher is personal to my uncle and meaningful to me. I refuse to share it with the world. If that's a dealbreaker, consider the deal broken."

"All right, all right," he said soothingly. "Let's not get carried away here. I understand completely. But could you do the translation by hand instead of typed?"

I frowned at the phone for a moment. "I *could*, but why?"

"Two reasons. First, if they're typewritten, any buyer will naturally be concerned that we were selling them more than once. They'll insist on being the only one in possession of the notes."

"I could see that. What's the second reason?"

"Well…" He was smiling. I could hear it in his voice. "The second reason is both true and deceptive."

"You want to market them as Charles Warren's handwritten notes."

"Which will technically be true," Mr. McDonnell said quickly. "They will be his handwritten notes. They just won't be in his handwriting. They'll be in yours."

"You could tell them that I translated his cipher."

"No," Mr. McDonnell said. "They'll want to eliminate the possibility of a mistranslation on your part. They'll insist on getting both the originals and the key."

"I read and write that cipher as easily as I do English."

"Of course you do. You were his favorite nephew. Which is why I'm comfortable selling your translation, and leaving out the detail that it *is* a translation. I'm completely confident in your accuracy."

"All right," I said. "Then after I translate them, I'll destroy the originals. So you can honestly tell people you're selling the only copy in existence of his handwritten notes about this hunt."

"You're willing to do that?"

"Why not? I have a great many keepsakes from my uncle. I don't need one set of notes about a specific treasure hunt."

"Tell me this much now, so I can get the process started. What was he after?"

"You mean you really don't know?"

"No, of course not!" Mr. McDonnell said. "Of course not. He never told me what he was chasing until he had it in his hands. Considered it bad luck to do otherwise. But in this case, he did say that if he found it, it would be the crowning achievement of his career. And that's saying something."

"I guess it would've been at that," I said, trying to sound wistful. "He was after a shipment of orichalcum that had sunk on its way to Athens. Fifty talents worth."

"Fifty talents," he said thoughtfully. "Why that would be…"

"Just under three thousand pounds of orichalcum."

"Good lord! That would be the greatest find since King Tut's tomb."

"And to be clear, we're not talking about the Roman alloy, that people know today. According to my uncle's notes, this was a shipment of the true metal."

"Great heavens!" I swear I could hear the big man leap to his feet. "Charlie, are you sure of this?"

"My uncle's notes are quite clear on the matter."

"But such a find would be *world-shaking*. And in that quantity…"

"Exactly. The crowning jewel of his storied career."

"His name would live beside the greatest archaeologists in history. And the payday…" He had to clear his throat. "Oh, Charlie. We shouldn't settle for a flat fee for you. You should get a cut of the findings."

"No," I said. "If this shipment has gone unfound for this long, there's probably a good reason for it. And these other treasure hunters, they're not my uncle. Maybe *he* could've found that shipment, but that doesn't mean *they* could. I'll take the certainty of a fee over the uncertainty of a percentage."

"You're sure? You could be part of history."

"I don't want to be a treasure hunter," I said. "I don't want to invest in treasure hunters. And I certainly don't want to partner with one."

"But if they find it, you could be losing out on—"

"Mr. McDonnell," I said, letting all the exhaustion of my recent travels show in my voice, "my uncle has already left me more money than I could spend in one lifetime. I agree that he would want me to sell these maps and notes. So let's just sell them, and be done with it."

"All right," he said, clearly thinking. "I'll push for a higher up-front fee then, since there'll be no percentage on the back end. But the buyer will likely need to find investors to raise that kind of capital..."

"Fortunately," I said, "I have a good agent in this matter."

"You do indeed," he said, with a chuckle. "I'll get you a good deal, Charlie. You can trust me on that."

"And what did you have in mind for your compensation?"

"I was thinking two-and-a-half percent."

"Make it five," I said. "You've been good to my uncle and me."

"Thank you," he said, surprised.

"You're quite welcome, Mr. McDonnell. And thank you for all your help. I'll get started on those notes."

"And I'll get started on selling them."

"Still need to send the runner for the maps?"

"No," he said. "I think you've given me enough to get things started. Just let me know when the notes are ready, and I'll collect them all at once."

"You'll hear from me soon."

I worked day and night, translating those notes into reasonably legible handwritten English. I took breaks only for food, sleep, exercise, and my rituals. Didn't even have lunch with Becky until after I was finished.

That might sound extreme, but I wanted this part done. Felt as though, once I sold off those notes and maps, I'd be closing a door that needed to be closed.

My uncle's legacy would be sealed, one way or the other.

And I played it straight. Translated the notes verbatim. No sabotage, tempting as it might've felt to lower the chances of anyone else getting their hands on real orichalcum, now that I knew what could be done with it.

But no. That would've been wrong. If I was going to sell these notes and maps, then I was going to sell them just as they were and let the chips fall where they may.

Took me close to three-and-a-half days, in all. Handed the whole package off to Mr. McDonnell's runner on a late Saturday afternoon in early January. Burned the originals in the fireplace that evening.

He got a bidding war going among the major players in the treasure hunting world. Gave me updates every couple of days. Finally completed the sale in early February.

Damn near doubled my net worth. Have to admit, though. Even that price tag was nowhere near the value of even a half-pound of orichalcum, in the right hands.

Still, I was more than happy with the results. Made plans to buy rainforest and invest in certain ecological charities, once I figured out how to do such things without drawing attention.

Then it was just a matter of making clear to Mr. McDonnell that I would be keeping my uncle's grimoires, and I was pretty much done with him. Unless I needed any legal work, somewhere down the line.

For now, though, that part was over.

My college studies gained a new focus. I wouldn't major in Business after all. I'd study Linguistics instead. Get at least a Bachelor's, and decide what to do from there.

On the side, I'd continue my study of magic, and start working my way through the garage. Learning more about the sorts of truths that had fallen between the cracks of modern modes of thought.

If Immortality was real, what else could be?

SIGN UP FOR STEFON'S NEWSLETTER

Stefon loves to keep in touch with his readers, and loves to keep you reading. The best way for him to do both is for you to sign up for his newsletter.

Sign up at http://www.stefonmears.com/join

If you sign up for Stefon's newsletter, you get...

- Monthly updates about his publishing and travel schedules
- His latest news, in brief, and answers to reader questions
- A free short story for signing up
- List-only offers and occasional specials
- Plus a free short story every month!

ABOUT THE AUTHOR

Stefon Mears has discovered some strange things in garages. Stefon has more than thirty books to his credit, and he never stops writing. He earned his M.F.A. in Creative Writing from N.I.L.A., and his B.A. in Religious Studies (double emphasis in Ritual and Mythology) from U.C. Berkeley. He's a lifelong gamer and fantasy fan. Stefon lives in Portland, Oregon, with his wife and three cats.

Look for Stefon online:
www.stefonmears.com
himself@stefonmears.com

ALSO BY STEFON MEARS

Cavan Oltblood Series

Half a Wizard

The Ice Dagger

The Spell in the Blade

Spells for Hire

Devil's Shoestring

Zombie Powder

Spirit Trap

Dragon's Blood

The Rise of Magic

Magician's Choice

Sleight of Mind

Lunar Alchemy

Three Fae Monte

The Sphinx Principle

Double Backed Magic

The Telepath Trilogy

Surviving Telepathy

Immoral Telepathy

Targeting Telepathy

Edge of Humanity

Caught Between Monsters

Hunting Monsters

Power City Tales

Not Quite Bulletproof

No Money in Heroism

Standalones

Between the Cracks

Sects and the City

Prince of a Thousand Worlds

Devil's Night

Portal-Land, Oregon

With a Broken Sword

Twice Against the Dragon

The House on Cedar Street

Stealing from Pirates

Fade to Gold

Sudden Death

On the Edge of Faerie

Collections

Spell Slingers

Twisted Timelines

Longhairs and Short Tales: A Collection of Cat Stories

The Patreon Collection Vols. 1-7 (Vol. 8 coming soon)

Confronting Legends (Spells & Swords Vol. 1)

Uncle Stone Teeth and Other Macabre Poems

Nonfiction

The 30-Day Novel and Beyond!